UNDER *the* RADAR

RECASTING THE CHRISTMAS STORY IN THE CONTEXT OF THE SPIRITUAL WAR BETWEEN HEAVEN AND HELL

CLIFTON WELSH

This is a work of fiction. Names, characters, places, and incidents either are the product of the author's imagination or are used fictitiously. Any resemblance to actual persons, living or dead, events, or locales is entirely coincidental.

First paperback edition August 2019
Contact the author at: CliftonWelsh33@gmail.com

Book and cover design: Jack McNeil
Cover Image: Thomas Cole, *The Angel Appearing to the Shepherds* (1833-1834), 101 1/2" x 185 1/2"; Oil on Canvas. Public Domain.

ISBN 978-1-7334-6010-1

TABLE OF CONTENTS

INTRODUCTION

All humanity suffers in bondage under the rule of the ruthless Commander. Exiled from his own dimension because he tried to overthrow the Kingdom of the Prince, the Commander and his followers arrive as an alien force, quickly subjugating the human world and setting up their "Order."

Word reaches the Prince of the Commander's actions. The Prince marshals His armies, comes to Earth, and engages the Commander and his armies. In the ensuing battles, the world that was is destroyed. Faced with complete annihilation, the Commander reveals that he has corrupted humanity in such a way that the Order can be defeated only by driving mankind into extinction.

The Prince relents and withdraws his forces without total victory. However, He vows to return to Earth to liberate humanity and bring the Commander and all his forces to their final ruin.

For centuries, members of the Order work diligently to decipher the Prince's communications with His followers on Earth. The Commander must know when to put his forces on high alert.

Now they know the Prince is coming.

CHAPTER 1

THE MISSION

Merchants lugging goods to the marketplace. Crowds of men on various tasks. Women going to or coming from buying produce for their families. Occasional animals pulling carts, forcing the crowd aside to allow passage. Many colors. Reds, yellows, greens, blues. But mostly muted by the orange brown dust of the street. Unnoticed are two young men walking among the crowd. They are identified by one distinguishing factor. Their colors – skin, hair, and clothing – are shades of grey. They look like throwbacks to the movies of the 1940's.

They depart the crowd by turning into a narrow

passageway darkened by the shadows of adjacent buildings. The passageway leads to the crumbling façade of an old structure – a building that has seen multiple uses over its long lifetime and now, by all appearances, looks to be abandoned. The passageway ends at the base of two stone steps that rise to a wooden door discolored by years of weathering and striped pale grey by fungi occupying spaces between cracks. The two young men climb the stone steps and vanish through the unopened door.

Once inside, they descend two stone steps back to street-level. The floor consists of hard-packed dirt. The windowless room, lighted by oil lamps along the walls, looks large enough to hold a hundred men at least. A large stone pillar in the center of the room supports the heavy beams of the ceiling. At the far end of the room eight men are seated around a large table. There is an empty seat at the end. Standing around the table is a group of about fifty. All are shades of black and white. The two young men slowly and quietly approach the group.

One of the men (his name is G37) surveys the group. The eight seated at the table appear to be in the S and T class. Members of the Order are named by power and authority according to the alphabet (A-Z) with "A" naming the least powerful and "Z" naming the one with greatest power. G37's partner is G60. The name ranks each member of the Order by power (the letter) and by the numerical order (the number) when he joined the Order.

Most of those standing appear to be scattered in the H to R class. Notably missing are those in the U to Y class who were utterly destroyed to the last man in a disastrous battle with forces under the command of the Prince about twenty-four hundred years ago. Even the Commander (Z1) is said to have lost power during that battle. The Order never has regained its former glory, so strategies to rule have shifted from overt to covert tactics.

G37 and G60, being of the least notable class, are part of this meeting because of their skills. They are rovers, observers, or curriers so to speak. Their assignments are to gather and convey information from those whose assignments keep them fixed in location and report back to their superiors. They may also monitor individuals when necessary. Now eight of those superiors rise and turn to face the empty chair. Those standing fall silent and turn toward the empty chair also. Z1 enters the room. The nine seat themselves simultaneously. The meeting begins.

His voice is quiet but powerful. "I remind you who are standing that you are attending this meeting because you have been selected to participate in the Order's most critical mission. We know this: The Prince has plans to invade our dominion disguised as a human. Should He succeed, it could well be our final ruin. However, we have found one weakness in His plan. He must enter the human world as a baby. Before He can become powerful, He will be exposed to the actions of our operatives. If we seize the right moment and take Him out while a child, two things can happen to our advantage. First, we will preserve the dominion we possess. Second, it may be that the Prince Himself will fall under our power and that will open the door to limitless opportunities."

Z1 smiles. "S11, what have you to report?"

"My team, B16 (jealousy), C39 (paranoia), D1 (murder), and C20 (insecurity), has gained control of King Herod. They have tested their plan." S11 pauses for effect. "The plan works. Herod killed his own son. Herod is ready. We are ready."

"T49. Your report."

"We are updating our files on all people of this nation with particular attention given to those of the bloodline of the Son of Jesse. And that is a lot of people."

"And that is why you have been called to this meeting," interrupts Z1 gesturing to those who are standing. "You will work in pairs assigned to the villages and cities in accordance with population. You will monitor pregnancies. Your findings will be matched with the data assembled by T49. You will also be particularly attentive to the presence and/or activities of forces connected with the Prince."

"May I ask a question?" comes a voice from one standing whom G37 cannot see.

"Proceed."

"It has been twenty-four hundred years since the great battle. Why the urgency now?"

Z1 turns to the eight sitting at the table. "Why don't you answer that T7?"

One who is clearly a Master rises from his chair.

"The Prince left clues for His followers of things He planned to do and when. We have decoded these clues so we will be prepared for action when these things begin to happen. One of these clues was given by Daniel the Prophet five hundred and thirty years ago. He saw a huge statue made of four metals. The head of gold represented the king of Babylon. The shoulders and breast of silver represented the Medes and Persians. The remainder of the torso and thighs of brass represented the Greeks. And the legs of Iron represent the Romans. Then the Prince destroys the whole thing. Roman rule began about sixty years ago."

"Yes, but the clues don't tell us how long the Romans will rule before that happens. It could be thousands of years in the future," protests the questioner.

"There is another clue that gives us a more precise date," replies T7. "Daniel also told the Prince's followers that there would be sixty-three weeks of years from the time the order to restore Jerusalem was given until the coming of the Prince. That works out to within fifty years from now."

"And that should imprint on your minds the urgency of your mission," continues Z1. "It can be we are too late, but I don't think so. The Prince, if born today, will make His showing thirty to fifty years from now. But we must act now! You will work in teams. The number of teams who will monitor your assigned community will depend on the population of your community."

"Excuse me, Sir," comes a voice from one G37 can clearly see. He looks to be in the P class. "I don't mean to be disrespectful but there is something I don't understand."

Z1 nods.

"It seems to me the Prince can do anything He wants. Why shouldn't He disguise Himself as an adult human and come as a warrior? Why should we be marshaling our forces to stop this 'baby' thing?"

"That is a good question P3. It highlights why we have designed our strategy. T7."

T7 continues. "We deciphered another message the Prince sent His followers through the prophet Isaiah. 'For unto us a child will be born; unto us a son will be given. And the government will rest on His shoulders; and His Name will be called Wonderful Counselor, Mighty God, Eternal Father, Prince of Peace.' Those are names the Prince reserves only for Himself."

"Any other questions?"

Another hand rises.

"Speak."

"T49 tells us that particular attention is being given to those of the bloodline of the Son of Jesse. What is so important about the Son of Jesse?"

Z1 nods toward T7.

"The Son of Jesse is another name for King David who ruled Israel about nine hundred years ago. The Prince made a covenant that one of David's descendants will rule forever. The Prince has limited Himself to coming through someone of the bloodline of the Son of Jesse. Obviously, this self-limitation is to our advantage."

Silence settles over the room. Z1 turns toward the table. "S52, what do you have to report?"

"No angelic activity, Sir. All is quiet. Nothing has changed."

"Yet angels can move invisible to us. Yes?"

"True, Sir. We have detected no changes in power; no shifts of light."

"Very well. Meeting adjourned. Proceed to

your assignments."

G37 and G60 are back on the street. They dissolve into the crowds.

CHAPTER 2

DISTURBANCE AT THE TEMPLE

It is early in the morning. The shadows from the hills give way to direct sunlight over a cluster of houses in a village just beyond Jerusalem. In one of these houses in the middle of a small room a man stands at attention. The white of his beard climbs up past his ears to mix with a few strands of natural color. The skin on the back of his hands and on his face shows the mottles of age. He is clothed in his finest garment – a robe of pure clean white – and his wife examines his face to make sure every hair is in place. A voice cries from outside his front door. "Zechariah. Are you ready?" Zechariah relaxes. He pulls the old woman into his arms with a long warm hug then kisses her on her forehead. She glows. Then he turns toward the door as her smile slowly fades.

Zechariah is of the tribe of Levi and today is a day of honor. The Division of Abijah, of which he is a member, is on duty at the Temple. Zechariah has served at the Temple since the days of his youth. The Division is called up about once every three years. As he approaches where the road begins the ascent into Jerusalem, he figures he has worked the Temple about twenty times. His two friends slow their pace to stay with Zechariah.

In the early afternoon Eleazer, the High Priest, gives the signal and the sixty-four men of the Division of Abijah gather in a large private room across the courtyard from the Temple. A line is drawn on the floor. Eleazer enters the room.

"It is time to choose the priest to offer the incense. Divide yourselves into two groups of equal size on either side of the line."

After a few moments of shuffling the room is quiet. Eleazer produces a coin about three inches in diameter. One side is colored white and the other side is colored black.

"Those of you on my left side are black and those of you on my right side are white. I will toss the coin and those not of the color of the side that comes up are dismissed to continue your duties."

Eleazer tosses the coin. It lands on the stone floor with a "clink." The white side is up and thirty-two men quickly and quietly depart the room. The thirty-two men remaining divide into two groups of sixteen and the coin is tossed again. It comes up white and sixteen men depart the room. Zechariah follows his two friends to the opposite side and the coin is tossed. It comes up black. Eight men depart the room. His heart flutters. In all his years of taking part in the casting of the lot, Zechariah has never lasted this far. His group divides, now four men on a side.

"Clink." The coin bounces, twirls briefly like a top, and spins down. Black. His two friends step to the white side. "Clink." Black again. Zechariah closes his eyes and offers a prayer. *Lord God. If your lot comes to me, I will serve You with all my heart.* Clink. After a moment Zechariah opens his eyes. The other man is gone.

"Come," beckons Eleazer. "Let's get ready."

The two men cross the courtyard to a small room adjacent to the Temple. There Zechariah is outfitted in garments of a priest. The pants are made of white linen as is the tunic. The hat is a long strip of fabric to be wound around the head. The belt is woven with threads of blue, purple, scarlet and fine white linen. The belt is wound around the tunic at his waist and the two ends tied in front with the remaining ends hanging down. Three other men had followed Zechariah into the fitting room. Two are dressed as is Zechariah and will serve as "backup" priests. The third man is an aide.

The five men climb the side steps to the front of the Temple. The courtyard is filled with worshipers. A trumpet blows and those who are laboring in the service of the Temple lay aside their tools and step back standing in attention. Those in the courtyard fall silent. Zechariah receives a small vessel containing fire from the altar, a knife for trimming wicks, oil for the lamps, and a vial of incense. He ascends the first flight of steps to stand on a stone platform.

Zechariah's legs feel weak. He feels lightheaded. Above him looms the massive doorway into the

Temple – a place he has never seen. He fights the dizziness by forcing his mind to review the mental model of the Holy Place he had been taught many years ago and rethought each time his Division was called to duty just in case. He takes a deep breath, exhales forcefully, and climbs the remaining steps to the doorway. Zechariah disappears.

The worshippers in the courtyard fall to their knees with their faces to the ground. The high priest and the three men with him bow their heads. One of the men, the aide, begins chanting a regular cadence. He is whispering but, in the silence that sweeps over the courtyard, he still can be heard by worshippers in the first several lines closest to him.

At the far side of the courtyard two men, notable by shades of grey, lean against the wall. H346 and H524 are bored. They have witnessed the proceedings every day for dozens of years. With their bodies slumped and looking down they see the whole practice as detestable.

H346's jaw tightens; his eyes widen; his head jerks up meeting the eyes of H524. Power shift! It is coming from the Temple. They leave their station, making their way across the crowded courtyard, stepping around worshippers. As they near the front of the crowd they can hear the soft chanting of the aide to the High Priest. They have passed through the crowd and now stand at the base to the steps to the Temple. They can go no farther. That the Commander will not permit.

The chanting stops. Over years of conducting the service of burning the incense, the High Priest has figured out how long it should take to complete the task. By his chanting, the aide is keeping track of the time required to do the job. Zechariah is out of time.

In his mind the High Priest continues counting. *One...two...three...four...five...six. Zechariah is old. Perhaps he is moving a little slower. Nine...ten...eleven... twelve.* The power shift stops. H346 and H524 look at each other. *Fifteen...sixteen...seventeen.* The two men, the backup priests, are looking at Eleazer. *Twenty-one...twenty-two...twenty-three.* A slight murmur rises from the crowd. Will Eleazer give the command? *Twenty-six...twenty-seven.* Zechariah stands at the Temple door.

He is not right! Eleazer gives the command and

the backup priests rush up the Temple steps and help Zechariah down to the platform. Then with a force not expected from an old man Zechariah pushes both men aside waving his hands and pointing at his mouth. Someone produces a stylus and tablet. He holds the tablet steady as Zechariah scratches a message. The tablet is handed to Eleazer who is now standing beside Zechariah. Eleazer reads the message to the expectant crowd.

"I have seen the angel of the Lord."

CHAPTER 3

THE COMING CENSUS

G37 and G60 hurry down the familiar crowded street stepping around people and animals as they go. They disappear into the narrow passageway darkened by the shadows of adjacent buildings. Then they vanish through the unopened door in the crumbling façade of the abandoned warehouse. They have arrived none too soon. The eight Masters are standing. Z1 enters the room. The nine seat themselves simultaneously. The meeting begins.

His voice is firm and urgent. "We have received information that leads us to believe that the Prince has put His plan to come to earth into action. However, in a way this is good news for us. We are not too late. And we are not too early. We have put our plan to intercept the Prince into effect at just the right time. Our forces are fresh and alert. T33 will fill you in with the details."

Master T33 rises. "According to a report from our agents at the Temple, a Levite priest named Zechariah encountered an angel while serving at the Temple. They did not actually observe the angel but detected his presence by a power shift. The power shift lasted for a few minutes, so our agents concluded Zechariah had been visited by a messenger angel. Information received from our agents operating in the village in which Zechariah resides confirms the visit by a messenger angel. Zechariah's wife, who is long dead as far as fertility is concerned, is to bear a son. This 'son' is to go before the Prince in the spirit and power of Elijah to make ready a people prepared for the Prince."

"Hold for a moment," interrupts Z1. "T7. You have something to say?"

T7 stands. "We decoded a cryptic message sent by the Prince to his followers via Isaiah the prophet about seven hundred years ago. 'A voice is calling, "Clear the way for the Lord in the wilderness; make smooth in the desert a highway for our God. Let every valley be lifted up, and every mountain and hill be made low; and let the rough ground become a plain, and the rugged terrain a broad valley. Then the glory of the Lord will be revealed, and all flesh will see it together; for the mouth of the Lord has spoken.'" We believe the Isaiah message matches the message presented by T33."

"T33. You may continue."

"There are two parts of the Zechariah message that need attention. The first is the name, John. The child is to be named John. We can find no role for that name in any of the material we have decoded from the Prince's messages. Second, the message states that the child will be filled with the Holy Spirit while still in the womb."

Z1 continues. "This is where we need your input. What is the meaning of John? Are there any groups in Israel that use the name excessively? Or those who place significance on John? If so, do what is necessary to get information. We need to know who these people are, who their contacts are, and why the name is important to them.

"Now regarding the second part, the Prince has given us an opportunity. We will place the house of Zechariah under constant surveillance. We will know the coming of the Holy Spirit by the power shift. We need to know when the Holy Spirit comes and we need to know who is present when (or if) He does come. However, keep smart. A move of the Holy Spirit is always accompanied by angels. Be sure your locations are secure."

Z1 turns toward the table. "S52, what do you have to report?"

"Aside from the power shift at the Temple, there has been no angelic activity, Sir. All else is quiet. Nothing else has changed."

"Very well. Meeting adjourned. Proceed to your assignments."

G37 and G60 are back on the street. G60 turns to G37. "Any ideas?"

"Well, so far all we know is that an old woman is pregnant and sometime in the future the child will be filled with the Holy Spirit while in the womb. Let's make our way through all the cities, towns, and villages in the nation. See if there have been any power shifts. See if anyone turns up who is enthralled with the name John. We will end up at Zechariah's village."

About three months later G37 and G60 enter the village of Zechariah. After a brief search of the streets, they succeed in locating H227 and H624, agents who had relayed back to headquarters knowledge of the angelic message to Zechariah.

"How did you find out the details of the message?" asks G37.

"It was spread all over town," replies H227.

"By whom?"

"Elizabeth."

"Elizabeth who?"

"Elizabeth the woman who is pregnant."

"Zechariah's wife?"

"Yes. For a week she was talking about it all over town. Since then we haven't seen her."

"What about Zechariah. What is he saying?"

"Nothing from Zechariah," laughs H624. "He was stricken mute by the angel."

"Know the name of the angel?"

"Gabriel."

"Gabriel!! Must have been having a bad day!"

Laughter.

Several days later, another of the G order, G166, finds the group. Without salutation or expression he approaches. "The Commander has called you to a meeting at sundown tomorrow."

Again, G37 and G60 hurry down the familiar crowded street stepping around people and animals as they go. They disappear into the narrow passageway darkened by the shadows of adjacent buildings. Then they vanish through the unopened door in the crumbling façade of the abandoned warehouse. Others arrive after them; they have not arrived late. The eight Masters take their places then stand as Z1 enters the room. The nine seat themselves simultaneously. Z1 opens the meeting.

"You may recall from our first meeting that one of your assignments is to monitor pregnancies and that your findings will be matched with the data assembled by T49. It is particularly important that we do this for those of the bloodline of the Son of Jesse. We now have information that should make your task easier."

With that Z1 turns and nods to one of the Masters

seated at the table. T24 rises to speak.

"Our operatives in Rome have informed us of a message on its way to Quirinius the governor of Syria. Caesar has decided to take a census of his empire. Everyone must register in his home city. That means a lot of people will be on the move, so the registration will take place over the period of a year. Those of the bloodline of the Son of Jesse will all have to register in Bethlehem."

"That means we will increase our presence in Bethlehem," continues Z1. "This will come as Caesar's orders are implemented. Any questions?"

Silence. Z1 turns toward the table. "S52, what do you have to report?"

"No angelic activity, Sir. All is quiet. Nothing has changed."

"Very well. Meeting adjourned. Proceed to your assignments."

G37 and G60 are back on the street.

CHAPTER 4

BEHOLD THE FORERUNNER

H99 and H307 are watching traffic creep along a Galilean road from a vantage point on a hill about two-hundred feet high. A few people walking individually; fewer people walking in small groups; all carrying loads of some size on their backs; here and there a donkey-pulled cart. They had spent the morning and early afternoon monitoring activities in the village of Nazareth, widely regarded as a "backwater" of Israel. They heard of the incidents at the Temple and at the village of Zechariah. They know of plans to increase the Order's presence at Bethlehem. Activities had slowed during the heat of the afternoon in the town where nothing happens anyway so they wandered up the hill a short distance from town to monitor the goings-on on the road below Nazareth.

"Power shift!!" they yell to each other almost simultaneously. "It's coming from the direction of town," yells H307. They take off running. Their trek takes them over grassy slopes of the hill which grade slowly down about fifty feet to a shallow drainage then up somewhat steeper to where there begins a narrow trail back to town. The trail leads along a ridge for some distance before it widens into a useable walking path behind a saw mill at the edge of town. They run past the saw mill, past a carpenter shop, and then past the stonemason's shop to where the path widens into a street. Their trek takes them past more shops and other dwellings and into the market place. They run through the mostly empty market place and stop abruptly on reaching the other side.

"It's gone! The power shift is gone!" huffs H307. It's something H99 already knows.

"Where do you think it was?"

"I think it was located somewhere in this quarter of town," replies H99 as he sweeps his arm from his left side to his front. It is an area occupied by the larger and better houses of Nazareth.

Almost three months have passed when G37 and G60 return to the village where Zechariah lives. They search out their comrades, H227 and H624, and find them hiding under a tree next to a stone wall. They are not directly across the street from the Zechariah dwelling as before but are up the street as far as they can be and still have a commanding view of the house. They have taken seriously the advice of Z1 that angelic activity could increase when (or if) the Holy Spirit came into Elizabeth's womb.

"Anything interesting happen while we were absent?"

"No. Elizabeth hasn't been seen since the first week. Some say she has fallen ill."

"She is an old woman. Maybe she needs her rest."

"There have been a lot of visitors. Mostly relatives."

"Who is that coming to the house now?"

H227 studies the man and woman approaching the door of the house. "The man is a brother of Zechariah and the woman is his wife. They are Levites." They stay for about half an hour and then depart.

Later that afternoon three men riding a cart pulled

by a donkey stop next to the Zechariah dwelling. One man, the driver, stays in his place while the other two men climb off their seats to help a young woman off the cart. Then they escort her and a bag to the door of the house.

"Who is the girl?" queries G37.

"Don't know," replies H227. "Never seen her before."

The girl disappears inside. G37 studies the cart as it slowly approaches then passes their location. Such a small cart yet such a long shadow it casts in the late afternoon sun. G37 grimaces as the shadow disappears, then reappears. He turns to see dazzling fingers of light fading from the eaves of Zechariah's dwelling. The surprise of it pushes the four back against the wall. Or is it fear? About two thirds of H624 has disappeared into the wall.

"Wow! That is the closest I have ever come to a power shift!" exclaims G60.

"That was more than a power shift," answers H227. "That was the Holy Spirit. He has come!"

G37's expression dissolves from awestruck to pensive. "We have to find out who that girl is."

“The cart is stopped by the town tavern. Ale flows freely there. The men will soon be talking. I will find out what I can,” volunteers H227.

The remaining three continue their surveillance of the Zechariah dwelling. Nothing else happens.

Several hours after dark, H227 returns. “The men are from Nazareth and the girl is a relative.”

G37 frowns. “Nazareth? She is a Levite?”

“No, she is not a Levite. She is from the bloodline of the Son of Jesse.”

Not much happens for the next three months. Elizabeth is not seen. Zechariah is not seen. The girl from Nazareth is not seen. There is a constant stream of visitors – mostly women bearing baskets of food. Except for the visitors, nothing changes. It is like a painting that once painted is always the same. Or a sequence of paintings to account for the growth and shrinkage of shadows during the course of the day.

To their relief, finally, late in one afternoon, there appears at the end of the street a donkey. It is pulling a cart, and on the cart sit the driver and two other men. Slowly the cart approaches. Then it passes by the four observers, casting a long shadow in the late afternoon sun. It rattles to a stop in front of the village tavern.

Early the following morning while the village is still hidden in shadows cast by distant hills, the donkey and cart reappear in front of the village tavern. After a brief delay, the cart comes slowly down the street and stops in front of the Zechariah dwelling. The two men climb down from the cart and walk to the door. They escort the girl from Nazareth with her bag back to the cart, help her on, close the gate, climb into their seats, and slowly disappear down the street.

About a week later around mid-morning several women come to the house. Then, as the shadows lessen at midday, one woman leaves in haste. Not much later she returns with three other women carrying baskets. Toward evening they leave chattering excitedly. G60 follows them up the street. He returns shortly, walks up to face the others, and speaks. "The child has been born."

The four observers retreat back under the tree against the wall, eyes darting around and upward. No sign of angels.

Eight days later a crowd gathers outside the house. A priest accompanies them, carrying articles necessary to perform circumcision. Zechariah, Elizabeth, and the baby enter the crowd. G37 leaves his location under the tree, slowly walks across the street, and mingles with the crowd. The baby screams, then cries. The priest raises his hand over the child. "According to the Law, I circumcise you Zechariah."

Elizabeth interrupts, "No indeed; but he shall be called John."

"But there is no one among your ancestors or relatives named John."

Uncharacteristically, Elizabeth is firm. "He shall be called John."

The priest turns toward Zechariah, shrugs his shoulders, holds out his hands palms up. Zechariah holds out his left hand and presses his right hand first finger into the palm of his left hand. Someone runs into the house and returns with a tablet. Zechariah writes on the tablet and hands it to the priest. "His name is John."

G37 draws back a step. Zechariah is speaking!

"Blessed be the Lord God of Israel, for He has visited us and accomplished redemption for His people, and has raised up a horn of salvation for us. In the house of David His servant – as He spoke by the mouths of His holy prophets from of old – 'Salvation from our enemies and from the hand of those who hate us,' to show mercy toward our fathers, and to remember His holy covenant – the oath which He swore to our father Abraham – to grant us that we, being rescued from the hand of our enemies, might serve Him without fear, in holiness and righteousness before Him all our days. And you, child, will be called the prophet of the Most High; for you will go on before the Lord to prepare His ways; to give to His people the knowledge of salvation by the forgiveness of their sins, because of the tender mercy of our God with which the Sunrise from on high will visit us, to shine upon those who sit in darkness and the shadow of death, to guide our feet into the way of peace."

G37 trembles as he turns away from the crowd now cheering in elation and returns to his comrades. "House of David," he murmurs. "House of David! We must go to Nazareth to find out more about that girl. But first we must go to Jerusalem and talk to the Masters. Some questions need answers."

CHAPTER 5

THE PARIAH OF NAZARETH

G37 and G60 make their way back to the abandoned warehouse in Jerusalem. T49 is unavailable for a meeting but his aid, J9, proves helpful. J9 confides the records are not as detailed as to give names of children in each family.

"One more question," pleads G37. "Can you tell me the number of families dwelling in Nazareth who are of the bloodline of the Son of Jesse?"

"Let's see," mumbles J9. "Oh, it looks like Nazareth has many Davidites. We have twenty-six families listed as dwelling there and I doubt the records are complete."

G37 turns to leave. "Oh, by the way," offers J9. "I

don't think this is a violation of protocol since we're all on the same project. You may not know this but there was a power shift in Nazareth about three, three-and-a-half months ago."

Two weeks later, H99 and H307 are back on the hill outside Nazareth watching traffic creep along the Galilean road. As usual a few people walking individually; fewer people walking in small groups; all carrying loads of some size on their backs; here and there a cart pulled by a donkey. Then they spot two men in shades of grey coming along the road. "Company coming," says H99. "Let's get back to town."

They meet G37 and G60 in the market place. After an exchange of pleasantries, G37 begins asking questions. "I learned from Headquarters of a report from you of a power shift about four months ago."

"Yes," replies H99. "It occurred while we were at the far edge of town. We were not able to get back in time to determine the exact location."

"How long did the power shift last?"

"A minute. Maybe less."

"Messenger angel?"

"That's what we believe."

"Follow me over this way," offers H307. The four agents walk slowly through the market place to where H99 and H307 had stopped running when the power shift ceased. "This is where we were when the power shift stopped. We think it occurred somewhere over this area of town," as he sweeps his left arm.

"Let's walk the streets," offers G37. "Perhaps we will find something out of place."

It is already hot for early afternoon. Few people will be about. That will make their task easier.

"This looks to be the prosperous part of town," muses G37 as they walk slowly up the first street. "Houses are fairly close together but are separated by well-maintained stone walls. Ornate metal gates."

They reach the end of the first street, cross a grassy field to the second street, and turn on it to come back into town. They go a short distance when G37 raises his hand and they stop.

"Look about three houses down on the left. There is a woman standing at the gate."

"Seems to be holding a basket on her arm," offers H99. "Probably on her way to the market."

"She's either waiting for someone to meet her or

she's looking to see if anyone notices her presence. Let's follow her."

After a few moments the woman turns and begins walking toward the center of town, toward the market place.

G37's hunch is correct. The woman walks to the center of town but instead of turning into the market place, she turns toward a cluster of dwellings in a less prosperous part of town. She turns down a rutted cluttered street and stops in front of a tiny dwelling. After she stands there for a few moments a girl comes out of the dwelling. She runs up to the woman who gives her a hug with her unoccupied arm. The woman hands the basket to the girl who quickly pulls out three loaves of bread and hands the basket back to the woman. They chat briefly, hug again, and the woman departs.

"Who is that girl?" queries G37.

"Wellll," sneers H99. "Say 'hello' to 'Mary, the Pariah of Nazareth'. She left town a few weeks ago and came back pregnant. Her father really went ballistic when she got back. No matter, she wouldn't reveal who her lover is. She even went so far as to implicate

God. That was it. She had disgraced her family and committed blasphemy. Her father disowned her."

"But the story doesn't end there," follows H307. "She was betrothed to Joseph son of Jacob. He refused to have her stoned and decided to marry her anyway. Joseph's father would have nothing of that. He wasn't about to share his inheritance with another man's child. But Joseph stood firm. So, Jacob disinherited him."

H99 continues. "Mary and Joseph; disowned and disinherited; disgraced and shunned; pariah and fool."

Both H99 and H307 laugh. "Haw, haw, haw, hee, hee."

G37 is not laughing. Is there a connection between the girl who came out of this tiny hovel and the girl he saw entering Zechariah's house? It is hard to tell. The girl he saw in Zechariah's village was tall, robust, and confident. The Nazareth girl is stooped, thin, and withdrawn. He can't even tell whether the girls are the same height. He turns to H99.

"What does her husband, Joseph you say, do to support her?"

"He has been trying to make it as a carpenter.

Has made enough to buy some tools and pay the rent I guess."

They decide to follow the woman. She returns to the main street and enters the market place. She buys some vegetables and returns home. Nothing unusual happens after that. Then the two teams part ways. H99 and H307 resume their duties as the watchers of Nazareth while G37 and G60 concentrate their efforts in the district where the power shift had taken place.

G37 spends the next month walking the streets of Nazareth within the area identified by H307 as the general location of the power shift that had occurred some seven months ago now. He observes that the woman with the basket of bread makes her trek once a week but not at the same time nor on the same day. If she is the mother of Mary, then Mary had been accustomed to a comfortable childhood. He locates the house of Joseph's father. Jacob is a prosperous businessman and head of a family that is highly regarded in Nazareth. He locates and verifies the twenty-four other families who make up the population of Davidites in Nazareth. J9 will be delighted to hear that the data he and T49 have assembled for Nazareth are correct and complete.

CHAPTER 6

ASSEMBLING OF CLUES

It has been more than eight months since the power shift at Nazareth. G37 observes that Joseph has done well at carpentry and has secured an animal. Although he does some work in a small open space behind the tiny dwelling, a typical day has him rising near sunrise, walking to the saw mill, loading his donkey with wood, and walking to construction sites. He returns home shortly before dark. Mary is seldom seen. On occasion she leaves the hovel to secure fruits and vegetables at the market. She is large with child. She seeks no conversation with other women. Some vendors refuse to speak with her. It seems the high point of each week is the brief visit from her mother.

One day G37 orders G60 to remain on watch at Joseph's hovel while he goes somewhere to think. G60 reminds him that such an action is a violation of protocol. Agents are to operate in pairs at all times. "My absence will be no more than two hours," protests G37.

G37 finds a protected area among a cluster of boulders in the hills above Nazareth. *Ok,* he thinks. *These are the facts. Fact 1: A power shift at the temple. A messenger angel visits Zechariah with news that old and empty Elizabeth will bear a son who will be the messenger of the coming Prince. Fact 2: Against all odds Elizabeth becomes pregnant. Fact 3: The Holy Spirit comes on Elizabeth. Fact 4: A power shift occurs at Nazareth. Fact 5: A girl from Nazareth visits Elizabeth. This we know.*

Oh. A correction for the order in which these events occurred. Fact 1: A power shift at the temple. Fact 2: Elizabeth becomes pregnant. Fact 3: A power shift occurs at Nazareth. Fact 4: A girl from Nazareth visits Elizabeth. Fact 5: The Holy Spirit comes on Elizabeth.

Conclusion: After observing all twenty-six Davidite families in Nazareth, the girl from Nazareth who visited Elizabeth and the Pariah of Nazareth are the same.

Deduction 1: The coming of the Holy Spirit on Elizabeth at the visit of the girl from Nazareth is a coincidence. The girl from Nazareth becomes pregnant during her three month stay following a tryst with one of Zechariah's relatives whom she may or may not have known. Out of shame, the girl refuses to identify the father and invokes the name of God in the coming of the Holy Spirit as a defense for her weakness. The power shift at Nazareth remains unexplained.

Deduction 2: The power shift at the Temple is a messenger angel announcing the birth of a child. The power shift at Nazareth six months later is a messenger angel announcing the birth of a child. The coming of the Holy Spirit on Elizabeth at the visit of the girl from Nazareth is not a coincidence. The girl comes home pregnant and invokes the name of God because she is telling the truth.

H99 and H307 claim the Pariah of Nazareth left town as a virgin and returned pregnant. What if? What if she left town pregnant and came back pregnant? What if the coming of the Holy Spirit on Elizabeth at the visit of the girl from Nazareth happened because of the Child she was carrying? What if the child the Pariah of Nazareth carries is none other than the Prince Himself?

G37 shivers. *What if the Agent of the destruction of the Order – the Order to which I bound myself thousands of years ago – is before me? Somehow I must warn the Council!*

G37 climbs down the rocky slopes back to Nazareth to rejoin G60 in his watch of the girl. As he approaches G60's station he shivers. He slows his pace. He shivers again. Instinctively, through ages of training, G37 knows what is happening. He is being watched. G60 is just ahead. But, unexpectedly, so is G166.

G166 looks at him with forehead furrowed and eyebrows pulled down. "You are wanted at Headquarters tomorrow at this time. The Commander desires an update of your activities." He departs.

"Bad timing for my departure?" mumbles G37.

"No," replies G60. "Just another Project meeting."

CHAPTER 7

TO FINISH THE PRINCE

Merchants lugging goods to the marketplace. Crowds of men on various tasks. Women going to or coming from buying produce for their families. Occasional animals pulling carts forcing the crowd aside to allow passage. Unnoticed are other men – in shades of grey - walking in pairs among the crowd. As usual, G37 and G60 depart the crowd by turning into a narrow passageway darkened by the shadows of adjacent buildings. The passageway leads to the crumbling façade of an abandoned stone building and ends at the base of two stone steps that rise to a weathered wooden door. Standing at either side of the door is a sentry. They are large and burley and known to carry out their tasks as assigned by the Order with cold efficiency.

H99 and H307 pass through the door seemingly unnoticed by the sentries. G37 climbs the steps. One sentry (M4) grabs his right arm just below the shoulder. The other sentry (M187) takes hold of his left shoulder next to his neck. G37 stares straight into the eyes of the one who holds his right arm. *Show no fear,* he thinks to himself.

M4 growls lowly, "You have been reported in violation of protocol."

G37 holds his stare into M4's eyes. "As reported," he growls back. "But not without reason. Detain me at your own peril."

"Our orders are to detain you under any circumstances, G37," growls M187.

"Understood," returns G37. "However, the timing of detainment is at your discretion is it not? I have critical information to report to the Council. I will never be far from you. You can detain me after I give my report, if necessary."

M4's grip on G37's arm slowly relaxes. M187 lets go. G37 proceeds through the door.

G37 surveys the meeting room. Most of the agents assigned to the Project are present. Others are arriving. The Council Table is empty. The two sentries are watching him from inside the door. Then one by one the Masters enter the room and take their places. They are followed by the Commander. A hush sweeps across the room.

Z1 is standing. "You were selected to participate in this most critical mission because of your distinguished abilities."

The word "distinguished" pierces G37 like a sword.

Z1 continues. "When we began, we knew that the Prince has plans to invade our dominion disguised as a human. What we now know is that His plans are underway. The angelic activity at the Temple and the appearance of the Holy Spirit at the Zechariah residence confirm that the plans are underway. Zechariah's pronouncement at the naming of the child also confirms that the child is the Forerunner – the prophet who prepares the way for the Prince. What remains is to identify when, where, and how the Prince plans to bring Himself into the world. Therefore, it is absolutely critical that you use every means possible to uncover this. I should not need to remind you that we – the Order – face a win or lose situation. It could happen within days or months so you must be diligent."

Z1 turns toward the table. "T7, do you have anything to add?"

The Master rises from his chair. "The Prince left clues for His followers of things He planned to do and when. We have just decoded a clue that reveals more of "how" the Prince plans enter the world. We already knew of His plan to enter the world as a child. To enter as a child means to be born of a woman. Over seven hundred years ago the prophet Isaiah told king Ahaz that a maiden would bear a son and his name would be God-Is-With-Us. This means the Prince will deviate from His past practices of using old women to bring in His servants such as Isaac with Abraham and Sarah and John with Zechariah and Elizabeth. As usual the Prince is clever in His messaging. The word 'maiden' can translate as 'girl.' The word can also translate as 'virgin.' A lot of girls have babies. But a virgin? Now that is another matter entirely."

T7 sits down. Z1 allows silence so that his listeners

can absorb the gravity of the message. Then he speaks. "T49. Your report?"

"We continue to update our files on all people of this race with particular attention given to those of the bloodline of the Son of Jesse. Thanks to some of you, our records are now more accurate and complete"

"S52, what do you have to report?"

"No angelic activity, Sir. All is quiet. Nothing has changed. We have detected no changes in power; no shifts of light."

"Very well. One more thing. Over the past year there have been three supernatural events traced to activities from the Prince. The two involving Zechariah we know about. The third which occurred at Nazareth we have yet to fully understand. The floor is open for questions."

The room goes silent. Then G37 slowly raises his hand. Z1 turns his way and nods. G37 opens. "With all due respect my Commander, I think I know the location of the Prince and the identity of the woman who carries Him."

The entire room faces him. Z1's eyes are cold steel. Elsewhere eyes widen; jaws drop. G37 gasps. The collective weight of their attention almost cuts off his breath so he cannot speak. He draws a deep breath and continues.

"The power shift at the Temple was a messenger angel announcing the birth of a child - John. The power shift at Nazareth six months later was a messenger angel announcing the birth of a child – the Prince. The coming of the Holy Spirit on Elizabeth coincided with the visit of a girl from Nazareth – a girl who just happens to be pregnant with the Prince. I say 'just happens' because the Prince dwelt in her womb before she arrived. It was the presence of the Prince, not the presence of the girl that invoked the coming of the Holy Spirit on Elizabeth. After three months the girl came home noticeably pregnant and was called out by her father. As claimed by H99 and H307 she invoked the name of God, but not because she was trying to conceal the identity of her lover, but because she was telling the truth."

"And Joseph, to whom the girl was betrothed and who chose to marry and suffer loss of inheritance, must have come to know she was not an adulteress, but that the child she is carrying is someone special.

So, I tell you, the location of the Prince is the town of Nazareth and the identity of the woman who bears Him is known as Mary, the Pariah of Nazareth."

G37 continues. "I believe we can take Him out. I believe we can kill the Prince while he dwells in His mother's womb. She dwells in a seedy part of Nazareth. The place is dirty, unclean. We have the resources to do it. E19 has the resources to do it. She can be made ill. She can die of some disease. No one would know it was us. We can win this! The Order can win this!"

"Look at it this way. If I am correct and if we take out Mary, we destroy the plans of the Prince and may, as our Commander has suggested, place the Prince under our power. If I am wrong and Mary only carries someone else's child; there is only minor collateral damage."

The room is frozen in time. Every face, eyes bulging, jaws dropped, fixed on G37. Then Z1 begins speaking. His voice is quiet and slow.

"If, as you say, this girl indeed carries the Prince, then she must be surrounded by angels, legions of angels. Even with one as clever as E19, I doubt we could get close."

Then the noise of a chair shuffling from the table draws the attention away from G37. Sensing the reluctance in Z1, T7 stands and faces G37.

"Do you think you have figured out the Prince's plan, G37? Do you see an easy connection between the girl from Nazareth who visited the Zechariah residence, the coming of the Holy Spirit, the power shift at Nazareth, the prophecy of the virgin, and the urchin on the street? For hundreds of years I have deciphered the methods of the Prince. He always operates in obscurity. He gives no dates for prophecies. His messages are ambiguous so as to be interpreted in many different ways. True meaning is open only to select eyes. The Prince *has* to do it this way, G37. The Prince has to fly under the radar. If He communicated openly, we would know His plans. We would be ready with our forces positioned for maximum effect at the right place at the right time. He would fail. No, G37, you have *not* figured out the Prince's plan. You have fallen for a diversion. Look through the diversion if you can and then tell us what you think you know."

Humiliated, G37 bristles.

"Still," counters Z1. "The idea does have some

merit. Enough to make a statement, but not enough to conquer a land. Swat a bee and be stung by many. Continue your surveillance of the girl. I want to know all that happens."

"T18," Z1 turns back to the table. "You may place your men at ease."

T18 looks towards the door to where the two sentries are standing and nods. They disappear.

CHAPTER 8

JOURNEY TO BETHLEHEM

G37 and G60 are back on the street in Jerusalem. For some time they walk in silence. Then, without looking up, G60 speaks, "I think he believes you. At the least I think he thinks you have a reasonable explanation for the events that have happened."

"You think the Commander believes me? I would have accepted more support."

"You got his support. He released you from the sentries did he not? However, I don't think the Council believes you."

G37 stopped and the two stood at the edge of the crowd. "What do you think we need to do, G60?"

"We need a 'smoking gun' – a piece of evidence that cannot be refuted by anyone on the Council, especially T7. But that is not all. In times past we bred monsters and sent whirlwinds into tents to kill humans. Now, to avoid the angels, we have to work through humans to carry out our plans."

"Like Herod, as S11 reported?"

"Yes. Not only do we need the 'smoking gun' but we need a covert plan to take out the Prince."

"Then let's find the smoking gun."

They turn down the road to Nazareth.

H99 and H307 welcome them back to their station across the street from the hovel of the Pariah of Nazareth then depart to survey the remainder of town. Late that afternoon the woman with the basket of bread appears at the head of the street. She walks slowly down the street stepping over ruts and stepping around litter. As G37 and G60 have observed before, she stops in front of the little dwelling. The woman welcomes the pregnant girl with a long tight hug then hands her the basket. The girl withdraws not three but eight loaves of bread. After another long tight hug they part ways.

At dawn the next morning Joseph's animal is tied outside the hovel. The donkey is already loaded with his tools. It looks like another typical work day. Joseph appears with more bags to mount on the animal; then one, no, two more trips until the animal is heavy laden. Then Joseph comes out of the hovel with a large bag that he straps to his back. Mary follows. Joseph grasps Mary's hand with his right hand and takes the lead of the donkey with his left hand. They slowly walk up the street and turn down another street that leads to the edge of Nazareth.

After Joseph and Mary have gone, G37 and G60 leave their post and cross the street. G60 leans through the door. The one-room hovel is empty.

During his long days at work, Joseph had been thinking. He was angry and hurt. Both he and Mary were rejected by their families. They were scorned by the citizens of Nazareth. In humiliation Mary was forced to wear the moniker *Pariah of Nazareth.* Joseph had a plan. He would work hard, harder than the rest; he would make money but spend little. Then at the right time he and Mary would leave for a new life in Bethlehem. Joseph was through with Nazareth.

It is ninety miles from Nazareth to Bethlehem. The road they take leads them south along the Jordan River valley to Jericho. There are plenty of others on the road and that makes them feel safe. For small fees they spend their nights on private campgrounds. At the end of the fourth day they reach Jericho. The road turns west toward Jerusalem. Traffic is heavier and from time to time they have to move aside for the passage of faster travelers. Their progress slows. They have been walking for five days and the road from Jericho to Jerusalem ascends from nine-hundred feet below sea level to more than two thousand feet above sea level – an elevation change of more than three thousand feet.

At the start of the sixth day Mary is fading. She is exhausted, almost faint, and stabbing pains in her abdomen are increasing in frequency. They stop to rest. As they have used up most of their supplies during the grueling trip, Joseph shifts the remaining baggage on the donkey. Mary will ride the rest of the way.

By noon they reach the road to Bethlehem. The traffic lessens and the way is not so steep. Late in the afternoon, about two hours before sundown,

Bethlehem is in sight. G37 and G60, who have been following a short distance behind them, are relieved also.

Stabs of pain are increasing in frequency and intensity. It is clear that Mary will not make it through the night. They arrive at the Bethlehem Inn.

In Joseph's day an inn is a building with one or more large rooms. One pays for a space the size of a sleeping mat. So do others. Mats are placed side by side. Several dozen people might fill a large room. There is no privacy. Most people are strangers. For the most part, they have no choice as to who will be sleeping next to them.

Joseph, with Mary following, approaches a woman who seems to be in charge of the Inn. "Do you have any spaces for sleeping tonight?"

"Yes, we do have a few spaces in the large room," replies the woman, who is looking past him toward Mary, standing with eyes closed and very pregnant.

"Actually, I am hoping for a private place. My wife is likely to deliver her child tonight."

"I'm sorry. This inn does not have private spaces," the woman replies biting her lip.

Joseph bows his head slightly. The woman steps closer to him and whispers. "I may be able to help. There is a private place but it is in the stable below the Inn."

"But there will be shepherds," protests Joseph.

"No. My husband is a shepherd. There are a lot of strangers in Bethlehem now for the registration and some of them are hungry. My husband, along with other shepherds in the village, has moved his sheep far away, out near the wilderness, away from everybody to keep them safe and to create space for animals of guests. There will be no one there tonight. Move your wife and your donkey to the stable. There is fresh hay there. I will bring down some cloths and bands for your wife."

Mary and Joseph, along with the donkey, hasten to the stable. As promised, the woman supplies them with rags and old clothing. Stench, noise, dirt, and dung-cemented straw keep the place private. Still, the stable is open on one side and is a place where anyone, anytime; animal owners, drunks, thieves, can enter at will. But for Mary even these thoughts are fading. Joseph has found fresh straw and created a mat. Stabs of pain in her abdomen tell her the baby is coming.

CHAPTER 9

MARY'S VISION

Mary wraps the little baby in some old clothing and places him in the manger of fresh straw. He has stopped crying and quiet spreads throughout the stable. Mary slides backward a few feet, rustling the straw as she does, and rests against the rough-hewn log that gives main support to the roof of the stable. It is quiet again.

Mary hurts. The place stinks. She is exhausted, famished. As she closes her eyes, a vision of home appears. The fine cloth covering the tables seeks visibility under trays of food prepared for the feast. There is her father laughing with Joseph's father, Joseph's two sisters babbling with friends, both mothers loading the tables with even more delights. Her friends and kinsmen from the city are there - and there is old Elizabeth!

Joseph's father claps his hands and silence radiates from him to the far corners of the hall. "Hail Mary and Joseph!" Applause and smiles. The guests crowd around seeking an audience with her first born - a son. Waves of praise and admiration sweep over her. Proudly she appraises her audience on the distinctive features, so small and delicate, that made the sleeping babe hers only. She looks up and there is Joseph beaming approval. He is leaning to kiss…

A rustling in the straw a few feet away awakens her. In a few moments comes the stench of fresh manure.

A stranger in an empty, hostile place. A castaway, lost from her mother, spurned by her family, branded, unwanted, unloved. A tear forms in the corner of her eye. There is no holding it back. She no longer has the strength.

CHAPTER 10

BIRTHDAY PARTY

Somewhere, according to those few who have seen it, is a palace, immense and high. A boiling cloud surrounded by a rainbow of color so brilliant and beautiful that it cannot be described hovers above a throne, high and lifted up. A place of worship, a place of praise, of continual singing, echoing with adoration to the Lord God Almighty. On this night the palace is quiet. Millions of angels, unseen, hover about the throne. An archangel has been summoned.

From within the cloud a thundering seemingly shakes the very foundation of the palace. "Gabriel, has no one honored my Son?" Gabriel stands in silence, head bowed, unable to imagine a response. Looking through the windows of heaven they had all seen the birth and still the image is before them: the baby, becoming restless and whimpering in the straw; Mary, weeping with tear-drenched cheeks; Joseph nearby, seemingly brooding, head in hands, motionless.

The floor trembles beneath Gabriel's feet. "According to their custom, to whom does it fall to honor the first-born son?"

"To the father…" Gabriel's bowed head is slowly rising, his eyes widening as one with a revelation, the shattering of a veil that conceals a truth so simple that, once understanding comes, it seems the truth should have been known all along. His face brightens; his lips draw back into an ever-broadening grin.

The chamber thunders again. "Make it so!"

G37 and G60 had followed Joseph and Mary into Bethlehem and set up an observing site across the street and up a way from the Bethlehem Inn. They are behind a wagon that had been parked in front of a shop by the store owner. Two teams of agents had been assigned by the Order to monitor the Davidites in Bethlehem with particular attention to be paid to newborns. About midnight, one of the teams (H70 and H84) approaches. They had been present at the staff meeting in Jerusalem and recognize G37 from when he presented his ideas regarding the location of the Prince.

"We take it the couple you followed into Bethlehem today is the infamous 'Pariah of Nazareth' and her idiot husband," sneers H70.

"That is correct," returns G37.

"She had her baby in the stable behind the Inn," adds H84. "Wrapped him in swaddling clothes and laid him in a manger. How quaint!"

H70's face creases into a smile. "Not the most regal venue for the Prince, wouldn't you say?"

G37 seeks to change the subject. "Been other births in Bethlehem of late?"

"Lots of births. The town is full of babies. From what we have witnessed, Davidites are going to be with us for a long time."

Far outside of Bethlehem and away from roads filled with hungry travelers, about twenty shepherds have grouped together to guard their sheep. They sleep in shifts with those asleep ready to be awakened should wild animals or humans attack their herds. The sky is clear, dark, and star-filled. A shepherd leans toward one next to him and nudges him on the arm. He guides his sight skyward toward a cluster of stars. One star seems to be moving and growing larger.

H70 enjoys his dig at G37. But what has he said that is so profound? G37 looks at him eyes bulging and jaw dropped. So does G60. H84 looks confused.

"Power shift!" yells G37. "It's coming from behind us! It's on the south side of town! Quick!"

They run back and turn on a road going south. It is a short distance to the south side of town.

"It's not in town," yells G37.

"It has to be close by," follows G60. "It is very powerful."

"But I don't see anything it could be associated with."

In a moment the shepherds are terrified by a blinding light. For an angel of the Lord suddenly stands before them, and the glory of the Lord shines around them; and they are terribly frightened. But the angel says to them, "Do not be afraid; for behold, I bring you good news of great joy which will be for all the people, for today in the city of David there has been born for you a Savior, who is Christ the Lord. This will be a sign for you: you will find a baby wrapped in cloths and lying in a manger." And suddenly there appears with the angel a multitude of the heavenly host praising God and saying "Glory to God in the highest, and on earth peace among men with whom He is pleased."

G37 turns and grabs G60. "I have an idea. Run to the southeast side of town. Line yourself up with some object in a straight line between you and the power shift. Be sure to remember where you are standing."

He shoves G60. H70 goes with him. "Follow me! I know the fastest way to get there."

The power shift stays longer than usual. In fact, it actually gets stronger. Then it disappears.

H84, who has remained with G37, gasps, "So that is what a power shift is like."

The two teams reunite at the observation post behind the wagon. Excited talk about the power shift and what it could mean slowly dies down. G37 looks up and down the deserted street and then across to the darkened Inn. He is silently disappointed. The power shift did not occur where he would have expected. He has no smoking gun!

There is perhaps a ray of light in the eastern sky. It has been quiet until now. H70 and H84 slump against the side of the shop. G60 has joined them. G37 leans against the wagon. Motion at the end of the street which merges into another street catches his attention. Men, perhaps eight to ten of them, pass into view as they walk along the other street.

"Who are those men?"

H70 brings himself to an erect position. "Shepherds," he replies disinterestedly.

"They are heading toward the stables."

"Nothing unusual about that. Shepherds and stables have something in common. Stables are where animals are kept."

G37 looks on with interest.

"You really aren't from these parts, are you?" adds H70.

CHAPTER 11

UNDER THE RADAR

The morning sun has risen to where the cool of the night has nearly dissolved. G37 nudges G60. "Let's go."

"To where?"

"To the place where you were standing when you lined yourself up with the power shift."

G60 leads G37 down the street almost to the edge of town. Then he turns up a narrow walkway and follows it almost to where it ends. He stops at the corner of a stone wall.

"Here is where I was standing last night. The power shift happened directly beyond that pole yonder."

"This is what I want you to do. Walk straight from

here to that pole and beyond. Do not turn to one side or the other. If you come to a dwelling or other building, walk straight through it. Also for trees and boulders. Keep walking until you join up with me."

G60 walks away. G37 returns to the road heading south from Bethlehem where he and H84 had seen the power shift. He reorients himself with the direction of the power shift and starts walking. For awhile his path takes him along the highway from Bethlehem, then he and the road depart as the highway veers off more to the west. The elevation becomes higher, the land rougher, and the place more remote.

After about three hours of walking, G37 sees G60 in the distance to his left. They are coming closer together. Finally, they meet at the top of a grassy knoll. They are six miles from Bethlehem. The place is empty. No one is to be seen.

"Why here?" muses G37.

G60 follows, "Strange place for a power shift. Especially one so powerful if you figure in the distance from Bethlehem. Must have been a large number of angels."

As they turn to walk back to town, G37 notices

a brown lump on the ground. After bending to get a closer look, he looks up to G60. "There were sheep here last night."

It is late in the afternoon when they return to Bethlehem. G37 decides to check out the stable. Joseph, Mary, and the Child have vanished.

Joseph put his plan into action. He and Mary had lived frugally while in Nazareth and had come to Bethlehem with money sufficient to rent a dwelling. They move into a two-room house in a neighborhood peppered with young families. The two rooms are almost mirror images. The front room has a door and a small window that face the street. The back room has a door and a small window that face a walled-in back yard. At the far side of the back yard a gate opens to a street behind the house. Neighboring houses are constructed in much the same way.

With the aid of H70, G37 and G60 locate Joseph's residence. The street is mostly open with few trees or walls. With no available places for protection, they are forced to patrol the street rather than set up a fixed observation post.

Joseph is unable to find work. He spends more

time than planned with Mary and the Child. One afternoon he asks Mary a question. "Why do you think the angels came to the shepherds and not directly to us?"

"I don't know. Why?"

"Well, perhaps it was because God didn't want everyone to find out about the Child. Maybe He sent the shepherds just to cheer us up. Think of what would have happened if the angels would have shown up here like they did with the shepherds. Think of all the people in the Inn. By now it would be known all over Bethlehem, all over Jerusalem and perhaps all over Israel that here, in this little house, dwells an infant who is Christ the Lord."

Mary looks at Joseph. She is not smiling.

Joseph continues. "I think I have figured it out. There are people who are not happy about that. Remember the visit by the angel? Remember the time you and Elizabeth had together? Then, BAM! Disowned! Disinherited! Rejected! Scorned! The poorest of the poor! If anyone had come looking for the Messiah, we would have been the last they would ask. Mary, I think God has allowed all that has happened to us to keep us flying under someone's radar."

"What do you think we should do?"

"Let's not tell anyone about anything we know, about who the Child really is."

On the eighth day, the Child is circumcised. He is given the name "Jesus."

Their money is running out. Work is still slow. Joseph sells the donkey to pay the second month's rent and to have money for a trip to Jerusalem at the end of the month.

Jesus is now thirty-five days old. Joseph and Mary pack up Jesus and walk to Jerusalem. Their mission is to visit the temple to offer a sacrifice for their purification according to the Law of Moses and to present Jesus to the Lord according to the requirements regarding the first-born male child. As they are unable to afford a lamb for the sacrifice, they offer a pair of turtledoves and two young pigeons.

G37 and G60 follow. But as required by the Commander, they are not allowed to enter the temple.

Their mission completed, Joseph and Mary find a less crowded place on the temple grounds to rest. Shortly they notice a very old man with a long white beard and pure white hair approaching. They do not know who the man is but later they will hear his name is Simeon, a prophet of sorts, who is known to frequent the temple. Simeon stops before Mary and looks at her fondly. "May I hold the Child?"

Mary uncradles and extends her arms toward Simeon who carefully lifts Jesus. He studies Him silently for a moment then lifts his head toward heaven. "Now Lord, You are releasing Your bondservant to depart in peace according to Your word. For my eyes have seen Your salvation, which You have prepared in the presence of all peoples, a light of revelation to the Gentiles and the glory of Your people Israel."

Wide-eyed, Joseph and Mary look at each other. Simeon hands Jesus back to Mary. Then he speaks to Joseph. "You two have suffered on the Lord's account, yet have remained true. Behold the Lord is opening the windows of heaven and is pouring out blessings toward you."

Then he turns toward Mary. "Behold, this Child is appointed for the fall and rise of many in Israel and for a sign to be opposed to the end that thoughts from many hearts may be revealed. And a sword will pierce even your own soul."

Barely has Simeon departed when there approaches Anna, the daughter of Phanuel, of the tribe of Asher. A prophetess and a widow at eighty-four years, she never leaves the temple, serving night and day with fasting and prayers. Anna looks on Jesus then turns away, calling as she disappears into the crowds. "Thanks be to God. Thanks be to God. Our redemption is near. Our redemption is near."

Mary turns to Joseph. "Staying under the radar? Perhaps we should leave."

The next day, the first rays of sunlight piercing the window awaken Joseph. In a short time, two men are standing at his front door. They are searching for a carpenter. There is work to be done.

CHAPTER 12

MASTER OF THE STARS

Far to the east, in a land beyond the knowledge of Joseph and Mary, a man sits down at a table beside a stack of papers. These are maps prepared by his students. With streaks of grey in his beard revealing age and experience, the man is a teacher of the night sky and students come to him from distant places drawn by a curiosity of patterns in the stars and what they might mean. Many years ago, the teacher came from a distant place carrying a similar curiosity. He sat at the feet of a teacher who had sat at the feet of a teacher and so on back many hundreds of years.

Over the past six months his students have been

assigned the task of carefully mapping patterns of stars in the heavens. Some patterns appeared fixed and could always be seen at some time during the nights of various seasons. Other stars were not fixed. Their positions shifted in the heavens from week to week, month to month, year to year. Where these transient stars appeared relative to the fixed patterns and each other was believed to harbor special meaning. At least that is what the teacher had been taught and that is what he teaches his students.

Six months is one hundred and eighty days and he teaches six students. To lessen the load, he has paired his students into three teams. Each member of each pair is to draw a star map only when his team is on duty. Thus, there would be produced two maps per night, a practice that pits the teammates against each other to produce the best map. The teacher devised the method to preserve maximum accuracy. Furthermore, he decided that maps would be produced only on every third night. Thus, Team One would produce two star maps on the first night; Team Two would produce two star maps on the fourth night; Team Three would produce two star maps on the seventh night; Team

One would produce two maps on the tenth night; and so on.

Still that leaves one hundred and twenty star maps sitting in the stack beside him. And he knows it will take him a minimum of two days to study the maps even after he has divided the maps into two piles, one labeled "red" and the other labeled "blue," and has taken breaks to rest and think. For he does not simply look at the maps, he commits the maps to memory. He is a master. He has committed to memory the star maps of his predecessor and the star maps of his predecessor's predecessor – thousands of star maps. That is why he is a master of the lights of the night sky.

Early on the second day, the teacher is looking at a star map that is curiously familiar. He checks it against the map drawn by the second member of the team. The star maps are identical. He puts the two maps aside. By the end of the day he finishes his study of the remaining maps. He leans back in his chair and cups the back of his head in his hands as he faces the ceiling. He closes his eyes and relives the night sky for the past six months.

On the third day, after breakfast, the teacher returns to his desk for another look at the identical star maps he has set aside. He holds the maps for a few seconds, then his head drops slowly, his shoulders sag, and he slumps in his chair. He remembers the pattern. Looming next to his table and above his head sit volumes of star maps assembled by his predecessors, thousands of maps he has committed to memory. He closes his eyes and ponders, *How am I to find the match among the thousands of archived star maps? Hmmm. I have an idea.*

He rises, takes hold of the last volume produced by his predecessor and opens to the last page. There, on a page by itself, is a star map. It is a perfect match with the map produced by his student, the map sitting on his table. His eyes widen. He brings his folded hands up against his lips with his fingers touching the base of his nose. On the map in the volume is written a message. *This map is a prophecy given to the founder of our Order. On the night there appears in the heavens the pattern of stars shown on this map there will be born in Israel a king. He will be a King of kings and the world will be changed.*

The teacher scrawls a message on a piece of parchment then calls for a currier. "Here, take this to our master in the east." The currier departs with the message. Then the teacher scrawls another message and calls for another currier. "Here, take this to our master in the north." The currier bows his head in a gesture of understanding and departs. As he leaves, he unfolds and reads the message. "The prophecy is fulfilled. Our course is the great bend of the Tigris." There is written a day and a month.

CHAPTER 13

THE GOD CHILD

It is late morning and G37 is completing a casual stroll down the street and past the house where Joseph lives. He has been following this routine now for months and there have been no events of notice. The boredom of his mission allows him to think and be angry. He is angry with himself because he allowed himself to be intimidated by H70 the night the suspect baby was born. There had been a massive power shift indicating the presence of a large number of angels. There had been a small group of shepherds walking along a side street. They became visible where the street on which he and G60 held camp intersected the side street. Two seemingly unrelated events. But are they?

The following day he and G60 had joined at the location of the power shift six miles from Bethlehem. There was no one to be seen. But, at the time of the power shift, was there no one to be seen? While walking over the grassy knoll, he had found fresh manure – sheep manure. If there were sheep on that knoll, there were shepherds on that knoll.

The shepherds G37 had seen were walking toward the stables, and the stable the suspect baby occupied was one of those stables. The sheep were already out of town were they not? Because of the large crowds the shepherds had emptied their stables. They were out in the remote hills keeping watch over their flocks by night. So why were shepherds in town at that time of night?

Of course, it could all be coincidence. But coincidence is the reasoning of foolish men. G37 thinks of various ways to explain the events. But only one way makes sense to him. The Prince is born in a stable. The local custom is for the father to arrange the celebration of his firstborn son. The Prince's Father sends a multitude of angels to a remote hillside where shepherds are keeping watch over their flocks by night, having been driven there by the crowds in Bethlehem. There the angels announce the coming of the Prince. A group of excited shepherds returns to Bethlehem seeking sight of the newborn Prince. They come searching their own stables which they already know are empty of their animals.

During the last fateful project meeting T7 had admonished G37 that the Prince had to keep his plans obscure to avoid detection and defeat. The Prince had to fly under the radar. It could be that, with the shepherds walking down the street, the Prince had celebrated his own birth. In the process, the Prince had flown under the radar. Right under G37's nose!

Had he ignored H70 and followed the shepherds, G37 just might have secured the smoking gun. Instead, it now is not worth taking his thoughts before the Council and most certainly not before T7.

At Bethlehem Joseph returns to the routine of his prosperous days at Nazareth. He rises just after sunrise, has breakfast, gathers his tools, and walks to his jobs. Income is sufficient to pay rent, buy food and pay for other expenses. He is planning to buy an animal should the workload increase.

Mary is making friends. It is slow going at first because she has to get used to trusting other women. Mary's best friends are Rachel and Salome, who are struggling with the same struggles Mary is facing, namely how to raise their firstborns. Her other friends; Martha, Sarah, and Miriam are experienced mothers with newborns and who have plenty of advice to share.

Mary comes to enjoy the frequent group trips to the Bethlehem market. The women also work on common projects like fixing evening meals for their husbands. No husband ever discovers that on a given night five other husbands in the same neighborhood are being fed the exact same menu.

All of the little ones are beginning to crawl. It is great to have a circle of moms to hem them in. One afternoon, after chattering over a number of subjects, the conversation turns toward identifying features that make the little ones unique. Over the next few minutes the air is filled with statements like, "She looks just like her mother." "He has his father's eyes." "She has my nose." All the while Mary adds her agreement but says nothing about Jesus. Finally, Miriam turns to

Mary. "Mary, I see nothing of Joseph in Jesus."

"Oh, Joseph is not the father of this child."

Five women, suddenly stone-faced, look at Mary. Mary blushes, "God is."

Mary smiles. Then Mary giggles. Then all six women have a good laugh.

"Well," laughs Sarah. "I guess we can call Jesus the 'God Child'."

They all laugh again.

The next morning after Joseph has left for work, Rachel and Salome bring small cakes for breakfast at Mary's dwelling. After some initial conversation and munching on the cakes, Rachel explains that the women have some questions. "During our conversation about Joseph and Jesus yesterday, Mary, what did you mean when you said 'God is Jesus' Father'?"

"Well, we believe that it is God who opens or closes the womb, yes?

The two women nod in agreement.

"We also believe that we plant the seed and God gives the increase, yes?

The two women nod in agreement.

"Then God determines what features our children

will have, does He not?"

The two women nod in agreement.

"So, Salome, when you said that Andrew has your nose but his father's eyes, aren't you saying God gave him your nose and his father's eyes?

The two women nod in agreement.

"But suppose God gave Andrew your nose and your eyes and your ears, and your mouth so that he doesn't look like your husband in any way, would you still say that God gave him your features?"

The two women nod in agreement.

"So, what we are saying is that since God gives our children their features, aren't we saying God is the Father in a way?"

Rachel and Salome agree with Mary's explanation. They visibly relax and conversation turns to other subjects. Nevertheless, among the six women, the nickname "God Child" sticks. After the two women depart, Mary draws a deep breath, purses her lips, and slowly exhales.

The wind blows dust disturbed by horses, mules, and camels away from the faces of the riders. At least one hundred and fifty men, all armed with swords, shields, and spears, ride on horseback. They surround three lines of pack animals with at least thirty mules per line. But most notable are the three men on camels, regal in their appearance, dressed in colorful garments, riding higher than the rest, to whom and for whom the services of all the rest are directed.

They are the masters from the east, the chosen teachers of the ways of the night skies. For a week they had assembled at the great bend of the Tigris River with resources needed for a long journey. Now the journey is underway. They cross the Tigris and are on the road through fertile lands between the rivers. Their course will take them west to a crossing of the Euphrates River about two days journey away.

CHAPTER 14

THE PLOT TO KILL JOHN

G37 and G60 are back in the abandoned warehouse in Jerusalem. Z1 has called another meeting regarding the most important mission of the Order – the group assigned to ferret out information on the plans of the Prince to bring Himself into the human race. The entire usual cast of characters has assembled. The Masters sit at the table surrounded by lesser beings who have been assigned lesser tasks. Z1 stands at the end of the table.

"I have called this meeting because there has been a lack of progress in disrupting the plans of the Prince to bring Himself into the human stream. The last angelic activity occurred almost a year ago."

Z1 turns toward the table and begins. “T33, do you have anything to offer?”

The head of intelligence gathering for the mission stands. “Our operatives in Bethlehem report that the power shift occurred about six miles from Bethlehem over an uninhabited area. They also report that the power shift was unusually strong, implying a large number of angels were involved.”

Z1 turns toward the table. “Do you have anything to offer, T49?” he probes.

T49 stands. “Our efforts to improve our records on this people continue to proceed. Otherwise I have nothing else to report.”

“S52, what do you have to report?”

“No current angelic activity, Sir. All is quiet. Nothing has changed. We have detected no changes in power; no shifts of light.”

Z1 turns toward the group. “I find this report of major angelic activity over an uninhabited area to be especially perplexing. Would anyone like to offer an explanation?”

There is a long silence. Then T7 speaks. “With your permission Commander, I would like to address the assembly."

Z1 nods.

T7 rises from the table and begins. "I suspect the Prince has already, or soon will, successfully birth Himself as a man. The Prince always operates by devious means. This I have already uncovered from hundreds of years of studying His methods of communication to His followers. In this view I see the massive power shift outside of Bethlehem as just another of His diversions. And it even happened in an uninhabited area! It is a diversion! It is designed to keep us looking at places where the Prince isn't. His mistake is in the diversion itself. We know He is here or soon will be. We only need a key piece of information to pin Him down. We need a....a....a..."

"A smoking gun?" offers T33.

"Yes, that is it. We need a smoking gun."

Z1 allows a brief period of silence. Then he turns, slowly looking across the group. "Anyone else," he inquires. Then his eyes fall on G37.

"G37. At the last meeting you offered an opinion on where the Prince might have attempted to incarnate Himself. Do you have anything more to offer?"

G37 looks back into the Commander's cold steel eyes. He has to be careful not to overstep the facts he knows. He replies, "I agree with T7 that the circumstances surrounding the power shift near Bethlehem are troubling. I agree, but perhaps for different reasons. At this time, I certainly cannot provide us with a 'smoking gun'."

H227, one of the agents assigned to surveil John, speaks. "May I offer a suggestion?"

"Go on," replies Z1.

"There are a number of things we do not know. First, we do not know for certain the whereabouts of the person of the Prince. Second, we really do not know anything of angelic activity. Yes, there have been reports of power shifts associated with messenger angels. But messenger angels are of a lower order. We know nothing of the activities of warrior angels. I propose an action that may force the Prince to reveal more of His activities than He would otherwise care to reveal. We know the child John is anointed to be the forerunner of the Prince. We know where John is. If something unexpected happened to John, the Prince would have no forerunner. As T7 has noted, the ways of the Prince are devious. Perhaps the Bethlehem power shift was a diversion. Perhaps John as a forerunner is a diversion. There is a way to find out."

"Go on," replies Z1 in thought, his eyes fixed on H227 and his hand cupped over his mouth.

"We could send several of our strongest agents to kill John. If they succeed, the Prince has no forerunner. If the prophecy is true then the Prince will have to wait for another time before another suitable forerunner can be raised up. If John really is the forerunner, the angels will have to reveal themselves to protect him. Then we can know for certain the Prince is executing His master plan. If no angels protect him, then we will know John is just another diversion.

"Hmmm," Z1 muses. "The idea will require the Prince to show His hand. That can give us a strategic advantage. But such a venture will be dangerous to carry out. If warrior angels show, our agents must be prepared to vaporize in an instant. H227, what is your plan to take down John?"

"Elizabeth is old and weak now. She spends most of her time in bed. Zechariah has hired a keeper, a young woman who watches after John like a hawk.

John often plays in a pile of sand behind their dwelling. Zechariah has rigged a bell at the back door and has run a cord from the bell to Elizabeth's room. When Elizabeth wants something done, she pulls the cord, which rings the bell. The keeper brings John inside and tends to Elizabeth. I propose to bring two of our R-class agents to the Zechariah residence. They will be invisible. I will step inside and pull the cord in such a way as to convey extreme urgency. If my plan works, the keeper will sense the urgency, rush inside to tend to Elizabeth, and leave John unguarded for a few seconds. Then our agents can materialize and finish John."

Z1 stands motionless. "Yes," he muses. "This can work." He turns toward the table.

"T33. Do you have any objections to the plan?"

"Only that there is great risk. Potentially there is great reward."

"Then get me R87 and R91."

T33 nods. In a few moments two large, burly, and muscular agents stand before Z1.

"This plan must be executed with precision for it to work. The moment the keeper steps inside, materialize and go for John. But while you concentrate on John you must keep aware of any angelic activity. The moment angels appear you must vaporize and return here to me immediately."

Then Z1 turns to H227. "After you have succeeded in drawing the keeper into the house you must be in position to identify angels if they appear. If angels appear, then vaporize and come directly here to me. I know vaporizing takes a lot of energy, but it must be done for speed and safety."

Z1 turns to the thugs. "R87, R91, I am placing you in the authority of H227. Once you have completed your mission return here to me."

The next morning H227, having returned to Zechariah's village, begins his surveillance routine from the sidewalk across the street from the dwelling. As he walks, he whispers, "Ok, I am walking past the Zechariah residence. I will go down the street a short distance then cross over to walk back. I will walk next to the wall that encloses the yard. Then I will take a quick peek to see if John is outside playing."

"Ok, I am at the wall. Yes, John is outside. The keeper is sitting by the back door. Let's go through the wall here."

They are through the wall. The keeper can't be seen from their location but they can see John. There is no noise with the exception of faint sounds coming from John as he plays. H227 whispers, "You move to where you can see the keeper. I will step inside and yank the cord. Hopefully it will draw the woman inside."

Now inside, H227 pulls the cord. "Ding, ding." "Ding, ding." The woman stands up and looks toward the door. "Ding, ding." "Ding, ding." She takes a step towards John. "Ding, ding!" "Ding, ding!" She turns around quickly and rushes inside. "Ding, ding!" "Ding, ding!"

Now inside, the keeper rushes to Elizabeth's room. Elizabeth is asleep. The woman turns and rushes back toward the back door. H227 notices two faint flashes of light outside. A broad smile stretches across his face. Mission accomplished!

H227 steps outside the room and back outdoors. John plays as before, showing no sign of having been disturbed. R87 and R91 are nowhere to be seen. His smile slowly dissolves into concern. He whispers, "R87, where are you?" "R91, are you here?"

Suddenly there appear in front of him two large angels, one standing behind and to his right of the other. In human terms he appears as a handsome young man – dark hair, large brown eyes, a face chiseled like that of an athletic runner. His muscular arms are folded across his chest. Not so with the closer angel. His face is scarred and round as if the muscles that form his face had been cut loose and now hang making his face drop. His lips turn down at the corners with mouth slightly open revealing clinched teeth. He holds his sword in his right hand and is reaching for H227's neck with his left hand.

H227's face dissolves into shear terror as the angel wraps his left-hand fingers around his neck. Then "poof" and the angel's left hand encloses a dissolving wisp of smoke.

H227 reappears in the dark windowless room of the abandoned warehouse in Jerusalem. Surrounding him are staff and other workers of the Order. "Gasp, gasp!" T33 stands in front of him. "Gasp, gasp!"

"H227. What did you see?"

"Gasp, gasp!"

"H227. Did you see angels?"

"Gasp, gasp!" H227 nods in the affirmative.

"How many angels did you see?"

"Gasp, gasp!" H227 raises two fingers.

"Two angels! You saw only two angels?"

"Can you name the angels?" comes a much stronger voice. Z1 enters the room.

"Gasp, gasp!" H227 raises one finger.

"Then what is his name?"

The power in Z1's voice enables H227 to catch his breath.

"Gasp, gasp! Fury!"

"Fury!" Z1 recoils as if from a bad memory. The others chatter fearfully.

"So it is true," mutters Z1 as he leaves the room.

CHAPTER 15

THE COMING PERSIANS

Horten Albus is a centurion assigned command of an outpost village on the road east of Damascus. His mission is remote but important. He is the first line of defense and communication for the Roman Empire should armies from empires to the east rise up against Rome. The Empire can spare few men for these outer defenses and that is what makes Albus ideal for the task. He is clever. He can do more with one hundred men than what most field commanders can do with five hundred men.

The outpost village does not have walls so Albus and his men have taken maximum advantage of the rows of mud-brick huts to construct a defensible perimeter around the village. Aside from routine military activities designed to keep his men ready and alert for possible trouble there is not much to do. And that is exactly the way Albus would have it.

With unobstructed light from the mid-morning sun blazing through the east-facing window of his dwelling, Albus is finishing his breakfast. His five-month tenure has made him used to the quiet that typifies life in the village. So, he is quickly disturbed by excited chatter between his servant and another man at the front door. The servant hastens to the table where Albus is sitting.

"Sir! One of our lookouts reports an army of Persians approaching the village!"

Albus pushes his breakfast dishes aside and stands from the table, his chair tipping backward and falling to the floor.

"Sound the alarm! Rouse the men! Get them to their posts immediately! Tell them to take no action until they have orders from me!"

The servant runs out of the dwelling shouting. Albus throws aside his resting garments and dresses for war. In a few minutes he stands in armored clothes, chest plate in place, and sword at his side. He steps out of his quarters and hastens to the edge of the village. The road to Damascus does not run through the village but passes just outside. The entourage is now in clear view. Thoughts run though his mind.

One hundred and fifty men on horseback! Calvary! They can slice us into pieces in minutes! We are already defeated!

Strangely the horsemen are not moving fast. Nor are they departing from the road. But all that can change in a moment.

At a signal from one of the men on camels, the caravan stops. A single man dismounts his horse and walks toward the village. Albus, seeing the man, walks into the open, beyond the defense perimeter. His mind tells him, *He is bringing orders to surrender.*

The man approaches him and bows slightly. Albus speaks. "Do you know Greek?"

"Yes I do"

"Speak."

"My master is on a journey to the west, to Jerusalem, to pay homage to the newborn King of the Jews. He only requests water for his men and animals. He will pay for the water."

Albus quietly exhales and visibly relaxes.

"It shall be done for your master as you have requested. Tell your men to remain as they are. I will have water brought out to you."

Albus turns back to the village and orders his men to leave their posts and assemble before him. Then he divides them into two groups of fifty men. One group of fifty is assigned to gather jars, jugs, buckets, pails, anything that will hold water, go to the well and fill the containers with water. The other group is assigned to carry the water out to the waiting Persians. The entire operation takes over two hours. Some fear that the rapid draw of water will empty the well but it seems that the water taken is replaced by even more water.

The fifty water carriers return to the village. Then the servant of the masters walks toward Albus. He bows slightly and hands the centurion a small bag holding ten small gold coins. Smiling, Albus receives the bag then turns toward the messenger. "Wait here."

Albus departs to his quarters. He returns in a few minutes carrying a piece of paper rolled into a scroll.

"Here. Give this letter to your master. As you continue toward Jerusalem, you will encounter Roman garrisons. This letter should ease your passage."

The servant bows and departs.

At an abandoned warehouse in Jerusalem Z1, T7, and T33 are in conference.

"What have we missed?" queries Z1.

T7 answers. "After reviewing the information provided by our operatives and messages by the Prince to His followers, I think we know two things for certain. First, the clock started ticking with the birth of John. Second, the birth of the Prince takes place in Bethlehem."

"John is two years old," replies T33. What you say implies the Prince is already here, has been for up to two years, or perhaps not at all."

Z1 follows. "Even if we know the Prince was born in Bethlehem, we have no way of knowing whether or not He is still there. We have no plan of attack even if we know where He is. And after what happened to R87 and R91 in reference to John, we can only operate covertly from now on."

CHAPTER 16

GOOD NEWS FOR THE MISSION

It is late in the afternoon. Shadows are already settling over the temple area of Jerusalem. Soils around the main gate are cooling off. Six men come through the gate. There is nothing notable about the number of men. Larger and smaller groups of men have been coming and going through the gate all day. More noticeable are the differences in their adornment. Three of the men wear clothing affordable only by very wealthy merchants or royalty. Two of the men are large, muscular, and carry weapons. They are obviously bodyguards for the other three. And the sixth man is more common, someone who may be an advisor, a herald, or a servant in some way. But most noticeable are the questions the sixth man is asking.

"Where can we find the King of the Jews?"

"You mean King Herod?"

"No. The newborn King of the Jews. We saw his star in the east and we have come to worship him."

The consensus of the men on the streets of Jerusalem is, "We don't know what this guy is talking about."

H346 and H524 are just leaving the temple area after a day of surveiling worshipers. A small crowd gathered on a nearby street draws their attention. They overhear the words "newborn King of the Jews" and move in for a closer look. Someone suggests that since their mission involves a king, maybe King Herod would know. A few minutes later two palace guards join the group. "Come. Follow us. King Herod wishes to meet with you at his residence."

The two palace guards, six men, and some of the crowd proceed up the street. H346 turns to H524. "Go to Z1. He will want to know what is happening. I will stay with the crowd."

H346 follows the crowd up the street. They stop before the Jerusalem residence of King Herod. The two body guards are left outside with the crowd. The three men in regal dress and the herald are escorted into the compound.

H524 materializes inside the old abandoned warehouse. Moments later Z1 stands before him. "Speak."

"Three men in regal attire have arrived in the city. They are inquiring into the whereabouts of the 'King of the Jews'."

"Where are they now?"

"They are being escorted to Herod's residence."

Z1 turns to others standing nearby. "Get me S11! Also get me T7."

In moments S11 appears in the room. Z1 turns to H524. "Explain to S11 what you have just told me."

"Three men in regal attire have arrived in the city. They are inquiring into the whereabouts of the 'King of the Jews'. They are being escorted to Herod's residence as we speak."

S11 breaks into a broad smile. "This is what we have been waiting for. I must go and prepare my team."

"Go."

T7 arrives in the room. Z1 turns to H524. "Now

explain to T7 what you have just told me."

"Three men in regal attire have arrived in the city. They are inquiring into the whereabouts of the 'King of the Jews'. They are being escorted to Herod's residence as we speak."

T7's stare bores into H524. "Anything else we need to know?"

"Well, their attire is not typical of these parts. They must have come from a long way."

"Then how would they know that the Prince has executed His plans?" inquires Z1.

"They said something about seeing the King's star."

"T7?"

T7's brow furrows. He slowly raises his right hand to his chin. "A star. Hmmm. A star. Yes. In the Prince's messages to His followers there was a clue so cryptic we deemed it unnecessary to spend the time to decipher its meaning. One of the books of Moses gives an account of a dispute between Balak, king of Moab, and a prophet named Balaam regarding future conquests by this people. In the end the prophet proclaimed regarding the Prince, 'I see Him but not now; I behold Him but not near; a star shall come forth from Jacob; and a scepter shall rise from Israel.'"

T7's stare again bores into H524. "These men have seen a star?"

"Yes. That is what they said."

T7 turns to Z1. "That means the Prince is already here. A key question is 'When?' We must make sure Herod inquires of them when the star first appeared."

Z1 turns to G166 standing nearby. "Go to Herod's residence. S11 should already be there."

CHAPTER 17

DINNER AT HEROD'S

Herod graciously welcomes the visitors. "Come in. You must have had a long journey. Have something to drink. Have something to eat."

After weeks of traveling and living out-of-doors, the ceiling and walls of Herod's palace are especially welcome. Drinks come quickly. The visitors relax.

"The people say you have come this far seeking the newborn King of the Jews."

"Yes, yes. We saw His star from our observatories far to the east of here. Can you tell us where he is?"

"No," replies Herod. "But I know who can give you the information you seek."

Herod claps his hands and a servant appears. "Go to Eleazer the High Priest. Tell him I have visitors from afar who are seeking information about the Messiah. Tell him to bring along other priests and scribes as he deems necessary."

Food is brought to the table. Herod continues, "Tell me about your journey. How did you get past the Romans?"

In about an hour the high priest and his entourage arrive. They gather with Herod and the visitors in a room Herod has set aside for high-level meetings. Standing to the side and unnoticed by the group is another man dressed in shades of grey. It is S11.

Herod begins speaking to the High Priest. "Eleazer, our guests are seeking an audience with the Messiah, the King of the Jews, whom they claim was born recently. What can you tell us about His location?"

Eleazer turns toward a group of scribes. One of them replies. "The birthplace of the Messiah is in the village of Bethlehem because it is written, 'And you, Bethlehem, land of Judah, are by no means least among the leaders of Judah; for out of you shall come forth a ruler who will shepherd my people Israel.'"

"Bethlehem is not far from here. I will have one of my agents provide you with directions," says Herod. "If you wish we can provide you space to spend the night here in Jerusalem."

The herald translates Herod's statement to the three men. After a brief but emphatic exchange, the herald turns to Herod. "Oh no! Thank you for your kind offer. But we are used to traveling by night and we wish to complete our journey."

"Very well, go with my blessing."

The meeting breaks up and the High Priest and his entourage begin to depart. That makes it easier for another man to enter the room unnoticed. G166 approaches S11.

As the others leave, Herod beckons to the herald and the three men. "Please delay for a few moments. I have some more questions to ask."

The room is quiet now that the others have gone. Herod begins. "Please, the coming of the Messiah is of special importance to me and also to the people of Israel. Go and search carefully for the child; and when you have found Him, report to me so that I also may come and worship Him."

"That we shall do," replies the herald. "Thank you for your hospitality."

"Oh, by the way, when did the star first appear?"

"The star first appeared about two years ago."

When the men had departed, Herod summons his servant. "Get me the Head of Security."

When the general arrives, Herod speaks. "Send three of your men to Bethlehem. Have them follow every move of the three foreigners. Make sure your men are not found out by them. If the foreigners find the Child they seek, report it immediately to me. I want to know the exact location of the Child."

G166 returns to the old abandoned warehouse. "Success! I got to S11 in time. Herod asked the question of when the star first appeared."

"And what is the answer given by the Persians?"

"Two years."

"That matches with our estimation from the time of the birth of John," growls T7.

"And that means every male child two years old or younger in Bethlehem is suspect. Add to that how many children in the surrounding environs should the Prince have been moved," followed Z1.

Z1 turns to T33. "How many agents do we have in Bethlehem?"

"We have two teams of H-level agents. Also, G37 and G60 are there."

"G166. Go to Bethlehem and inform our agents there to expect company tomorrow."

G166 nods and departs. Z1 turns to T7 and the rest who have assembled and smiles.

"Good. Very good."

CHAPTER 18

BEHOLD THE STAR

During their journey, the three masters leave most of their entourage at Jericho. Only twenty men accompanied by needed supplies make the final trip to Jerusalem. Only six men enter the city gate. Now they depart the city and rejoin the others. They mount their animals and move slowly away from the few torchlights along the city wall, giving their eyes time to adjust to the darkness.

At its rising the moon is full and the light reflecting off the light-colored soil gives plenty of light for the masters to find their way. Their way takes them east from Jerusalem for a few miles. Then they turn south on the road leading to Bethlehem. Here the valley widens giving a fuller view of the night sky. One of the masters calls out to his companions, "Look! Over there! It is the star." Their joyful exclamations break the quiet of the night.

The star is in the south and a little to the east. It is low in the sky, perhaps fifteen or twenty degrees above the horizon. As they approach Bethlehem the star is at its zenith directly to the south.

Bethlehem sits on a hill that rises directly ahead of the road. As they approach, Bethlehem seems to rise up out of the ground ahead of them. The light of the full moon is sufficient to illuminate the tops of a row of houses along the slope. The lead master raises his hand and the caravan stops.

"Come up to me! Come up to me!"

Two camels pull aside the first.

"Look at where the star is. The star is at the rooftops of the houses ahead of us. If we ride farther, the star will disappear behind one of the houses."

"It looks like the star is resting on top of the house," muses another master.

"Look," said the third master. "The star is on the one, two, three, four, five; the fifth house in the line.

Perhaps the Almighty King has placed the star to show us where dwells the King of the Jews."

"Let's dismount and camp here for the night. We shall find the King in the morning."

The masters awake at first light and begin preparations for breakfast. As the sun rises they are treated to a brilliant display. Layers of clouds line the west like ranks of a giant army marching across the sky. The layers closest to the horizon are clothed in deep purple red. The layers grade through red and orange with the leading edges seemingly on fire. As one looks higher, the orange grades to yellow and then to white with edges looking like feathers dropped by some heavenly bird and now silhouetted against a cobalt sky not yet lit to the blue of full day.

As the masters complete their morning meal, traffic on the Bethlehem road picks up. Passing by among the crowd of travelers and unnoticed by the masters is G166. Shortly thereafter there pass by on their way to Bethlehem three men wearing identical cloaks of brown with white stripes.

So as to not create a crowd of the curious nor cause a commotion, the masters decide to send the herald into the village first to find the location of the King. He will go first to the market place as it will be likely that women who know about children will be shopping there. Then the herald will return to lead them to worship the King. As the herald departs on his mission a light breeze is causing the sides of their tents to ripple like flags.

Joseph has left for work and Mary is cleaning up around the house. Jesus is walking. She keeps an eye on Him although the house has only two rooms and is lightly furnished. There is not much trouble He can get into.

The herald is in the market place. "Excuse me; I am looking for the King of the Jews."

"Excuse me; have you seen the King of the Jews?" "Do you know where I can find the King of the Jews; we have seen His star?"

The herald is beginning to annoy shoppers and merchants. Some listen and then shrug their shoulders; others turn away with a grunt. The herald becomes more frantic. There is nearby a woman with three children who is standing at a stall examining fruit. He goes to her. "Excuse me, I am looking for the King of the Jews."

Miriam turns toward him with a smile. "Do you mean the God Child?"

The herald ponders *God Child; King of the Jews; God Child?* "Yes, yes; the God Child! Can you tell me where I can find Him?"

"I will show you where He lives."

The herald steps aside. Miriam continues with her purchase of the fruit. Then she steps away. "Follow me."

Miriam leads the herald to a house. It *is* the fifth house from the end of the street. Pointing toward the house she says, "The God Child lives there."

"Please," begs the herald. "Go to the house with me. The mother knows you. She may not welcome a stranger."

Miriam leads the man to the door and calls out.

"Mary!"

"Yes. Oh, hi Miriam."

"Mary, there is a man who wants to speak with you."

Mary stands in the doorway. The herald nods to her in respect. Then he sees Jesus in the room behind her. A surge of joy flows through him. He has seen the King of the Jews. Excitedly the herald tries to explain his mission to Mary.

"I am a servant of my masters who have come from a long way to the east. My masters have seen the star of the King of the Jews and have come to see Him. Please remain here. I will go and bring my masters."

Mary nods; the herald departs; Miriam shrugs her shoulders and heads home with her family. Mary looks after her, wanting to ask her to get word to Joseph, but Miriam is already out of earshot. She turns inside and looks at Jesus. "I need to comb your hair."

Six men walk hastily through the market place. The leader is the one who had minutes ago annoyed many of the merchants. He is followed by three men in regal attire. They are followed by two large men; one bearing on his right shoulder a large roll of rugs and the other carrying a basket filled with boxes. They disappear down a side street.

Mary hears the voice of the herald chattering outside. One of the large men puts down his basket and helps the other large man unroll and spread three multi-colored rugs. Then he places three boxes at the heads of the carpets. The two men step aside. The three masters position themselves at the feet of the carpets. A gust of wind tries to roll up one carpet, but a well-placed foot puts an end to that.

"Come. Please come;" beckons the herald toward the door.

Mary appears with Jesus in hand. The masters look on silently for a moment then fall to their knees and bow their faces to the ground. They thank Almighty God for having given them the privilege of seeing with their own eyes the Holy One – The King of the Jews. Then they reach for their boxes and present them to Mary as gifts for Jesus. Mary takes the boxes but does not open them. She thanks the masters for their gifts. The masters rise, step back off the rugs, and bow. The two men hurriedly gather up the rugs. The masters bow again, the herald thanks Mary, and the group departs.

During all of this a small crowd has gathered. After the masters depart, one of the onlookers calls to Mary.

"Tell us. What's in the boxes."

"I don't know. Children's gifts I imagine. The boxes

will not be opened until after Joseph comes home."

Dispersing with the crowd are three men all dressed identically in brown cloaks with white stripes.

Also standing at the edge of the crowd are G37 and G60. G37 slaps his knee and yells out a hoot. "I *am* right! I knew it all along! The son of the woman from Nazareth is the Prince! Let's get back to Z1. We have the smoking gun!"

Now back at their camping site, servants of the Persian entourage are packing up. The three masters are talking excitedly amongst themselves.

"We must hurry and get back to Jerusalem. King Herod will be delighted to hear that we have found the King."

"We cannot return to Jerusalem;" says another. "Look up."

The army of clouds has almost conquered the whole sky. The sun has been vanquished. Gusts of wind are tearing loose soil and blowing small puffs of dust along the ground.

"A storm is coming. We have to get out of the high country! If we can make our way down to the great valley and to Jericho by nightfall we will be safe there."

CHAPTER 19

THE PRINCE REVEALED

Joseph prepares to leave work early. His job on a dwelling on the south side of Bethlehem requires him to work outside. Several times wind gusts have snatched boards from his grip and almost knocked him down. He looks at the sky. Not rain clouds. In fact, the clouds are tinged slightly brown.

The two years in Bethlehem have taught Joseph a lot about how to get around town. A little-used path runs from the main road south out of Bethlehem to a short distance from his job site, then along the east side of town to the street where he lives. From there a narrow path more like a trail runs slightly downhill to the street that runs behind his house. Joseph likes to use this way home because it allows him to enter his domain through the gate to the walled-in backyard and then to his back door without having to carry his tools through the house.

Joseph leaves his job site. He walks a short distance through a grove of short trees to the path. Gusts of wind blowing through the trees make an almost musical sound, but that is forgotten once he walks beyond the grove out into the open. Dust-filled gusts push him along and Joseph is glad the wind is at his back.

He turns onto his backstreet. The slope down and the houses offer some shelter from the wind. Thin clouds of dust race past just above him. As he approaches his gate, Joseph notices a man standing near a gate in a wall across the street. The man does not see him at first as he busies himself to shelter his face from the dust, and almost nobody approaches from the direction Joseph is coming. As Joseph walks closer, the man does see him and steps back through the gate behind him. Joseph notices that the man is wearing a brown cloak with white stripes.

Joseph enters his house, sets aside his tools, gives

Mary a hug, and tracks down Jesus to give Him a hug. He notices the boxes sitting on the table, then sits down on a stool next to them. "What are these?"

"You won't believe what happened here this morning. A man came to the door. He said he is the servant of three wealthy men who live somewhere far to the east. He said they had seen Jesus' star and had come to see the 'King of the Jews.' Then a little later he showed up with the three rich men. Joseph, they bowed down and praised God for letting them see Jesus. Then they gave me the three boxes and left. Isn't that amazing?"

Joseph says nothing. He slowly rises from his stool and, head down, slowly walks across the room to the far wall. Then he slowly walks to the window overlooking the street in front of his house. He stands seemingly in deep thought as he searches the street. *Yes. There he is! Standing by a wall one house down. Same attire as the man on the street out back. The house is being watched.*

Joseph turns and retraces his path back to the wall and to the table. As he sits down his thoughts continue. *We are being watched by someone. We can't leave; we would be followed. We are trapped!*

"Honey, is something wrong?"

Joseph doesn't want to frighten Mary. Doing so at this time would be pointless. Turning to Mary he speaks. "Let's see what's in these boxes."

As Joseph pulls the first box to him, Mary leaves her post where she is fixing the evening meal and stands behind him. He opens the box and pulls out an ornately colored jar. He opens the jar then quickly closes it. "Mary! This is frankincense! This is expensive stuff!"

Joseph reaches for the second box. It holds a vial of ointment. He can read the writing on the front. Myrrh. He looks back to Mary. "Who did you say these men were?"

"They were dressed like kings. But not from these parts. They said they were from far away."

The third box is a little heavier than the first two boxes. Joseph opens this box and looks in. "Wow! Mary, there is enough gold here to feed us for at least a year!"

The third man dressed in the brown cloak with white stripes returns to Jerusalem. It is but a short walk to Herod's residence. "We have found the Child in Bethlehem."

"Wonderful! The storm is too violent to go back tonight. I will assign you ten palace guards. Return with them early in the morning as soon as weather permits. Arrest the family and bring them to me."

G37 stands before Z1. "We have found the Child in Bethlehem."

"Wonderful. Take your rest. We will finish this Prince affair through Herod."

CHAPTER 20

THE GREAT ESCAPE

Wheeooooo! The wind whistles through a gap in the front door. Mary and Jesus are asleep. Joseph lies awake with thoughts racing through his mind. *What is God doing? The gifts are wonderful but are of no use to us. This place is being watched from both front and back. We are trapped! Any attempt to leave and we will be seen. God, Jesus is Your Son. You are in charge of His life anyway.* With that he falls asleep.

Bang! Bang! Bang! Joseph is startled awake. He can feel his pulse in his chest. *What was that? It sounded like someone pounding on the door.* WheeoooooEEEEOOOO Rooooaaaar Bang Bang

Bang! *It's the storm. The wind is hitting the house and shaking the door!* WheeooooоEEEEOOOO Rooooaaaar Bang Bang Bang! *Wow! Never have I experienced a storm like this. The dust must be so bad no one can see! Or survive!*

Wait! No one can see! Or survive. Survival doesn't matter. Surely we won't survive if we stay here. If we can make it to the path at the end of the street we can escape unseen. But we still have to face the storm!

Carefully, Joseph pulls himself up in the total blackness, slides his hand along the table until he can grasp a small oil lamp. He lights the lamp and turns the light down low. *Probably unnecessary;* he thinks. *No one can see in here anyway.*

WheeoooooEEEEOOOO Rooooaaaar Bang Bang Bang! Joseph is in the back room. There are burlap bags filled with tools and supplies. The bags are fitted with straps so they can be carried on the back. He saves only the most used important tools he needs to start carpentry somewhere else and empties the bags. There is bread, several loaves of bread. Into the bags they go. And dried fish; in! Here are some old wineskins. They can be filled with water.

He touches Mary. "Mary, Mary, wake up! We must go!"

Mary opens her eyes. Groggily she sees Joseph's features in the faint light. "Joseph, what's wrong?"

Rooooaaaar WheeoooooEEEEOOOO! "We have to flee. Herod has posted sentries in the front and in the back. I saw them when I came home."

"But they will see us."

"No! The storm is so bad they can't see us. You see? God is making a way for us to escape."

WheeoooooEEEEOOOO Rooooaaaar Bang Bang Bang! There is a slight smell of dust.

"But we won't find our way through town."

"I know. But there is a path at the end of the street I have used many times, even in the dark. I think I can find the path with my eyes shut."

Joseph pulls down a short length of rope. "Here. I will tie this around your waist and pull you along. You can keep your eyes closed. Won't be able to see anyway."

"You get Jesus ready. May have to completely cover Him. Keep the dust out. I will pack the gifts and put the bags outside."

Joseph turns up the lamp so both can see. Both front and back doors are barred. He lifts the bar, opens the door, and sets the bags outside against the back wall of the house. Mary gathers a blanket and wraps Jesus. Then she wraps herself. Only her eyes will be exposed.

WheeoooooEEEEOOOO Rooooaaaar. Joseph places Mary and Jesus outside and ties the rope around her waist. "Stand here, I have an idea." He steps back inside, locates a piece of thin string and ties it around one end of the bar. He stands the bar vertically on a ledge near the hinge side of the door. He opens the door and carefully steps out leaving plenty of string between him and the bar. He holds the string up against the door jam and carefully closes the door tight. He pulls the string. "Thud!" The bar falls into the brackets. The doors on both the front and back of the house are barred shut. Joseph yanks the string and it breaks free.

They stand in a continuous background roar. The back wall of the house blocks the direct blast of the wind but they are still buffeted by turbulence from wind blowing over the house. Joseph puts his mouth close to Mary's ear. "This is what we are going to do. We are not going out by the gate as that will expose us to the full force of the wind and put us too close to Herod's spy. We are going straight over the neighbor's yard wall and so on for all five houses. Once we get past the last house, we will have to turn up the trail. That's where we will face the full force of the storm."

"I will pull you slowly on the rope. When we get to the wall, I will take off my packs and put them over the wall. Then you hand me Jesus and go over the wall. I will then hand Jesus back to you and climb over last. I will pick up my packs, you hang on to Jesus, and we will go to the next wall."

Joseph slowly pulls Mary away from the house toward the wall. The wind blowing through the gap between the houses almost knocks them down. The blowing sand and dust sting any exposed parts of the body. Mary draws her scarf up to her forehead and keeps her eyes closed. They are in a blinding dust storm and it is pitch dark.

Joseph reaches the wall and pulls Mary up beside him where his body serves as a windbreak. They communicate by touch. He sets his packs over the wall, then grasps Jesus, whom Mary is clutching close to her bosom. Joseph presses Jesus against his chest with his right arm while shielding Him from the wind and helps Mary over the wall with his left arm. Then he hands Jesus back to Mary and climbs over the wall. He picks up the packs, takes the rope tied to Mary, and gently pulls her to the next wall. They repeat the drill for the next four houses.

After the last wall, they inch down to the street and then to the trail at the end of the street. Joseph must turn south, facing directly into the wind. He closes his eyes and pulls his blanket up over his forehead, holds tightly to Mary's rope, and inches forward. Mary follows close behind, leans forward, and touches the back of Joseph's pack with her nose.

The wind blowing past their ears makes such a noise they can only hear a loud roaring. Several times Joseph stops, barely able to stand against the wind. They have reached the end of the street that runs past the front of their house. The trail widens as they approach the top of the hill. Eventually they hear a roaring sound louder than the sound near their ears. They are approaching the grove of trees where the path ends at the road south of Bethlehem.

The wind slows down though they are in a rain of sand and dust. But they face a new hazard, that of wildly swinging branches. Joseph clings to Mary's rope with his left hand and holds up his right arm to cushion the blows from branches. As they inch forward the wind speed increases again. The loud roaring is above and behind. Joseph, shuffling his feet forward, finds the Bethlehem road.

They have been at this for over two hours and have gone less than a mile. A trace of daylight is filtering down through the storm. Joseph lowers his shield to expose his eyes. Turning his face sideways to the left, he closes his right eye. Using his nose as a windbreak for his left eye, he can barely make out the edge of the road at his side.

They shuffle along the road for seemingly a long time. Joseph notices that along this stretch of the road the wind is blowing from a little west of due south. He is able to hold his head more forward to see further up the road, but not far, and it does expose Mary and Jesus to more wind.

The wind is slamming Joseph and Mary in wild

gusts and it is becoming harder to stand. The wind has also shifted to blow more from the southwest. Joseph has no idea what time it is but it is getting lighter. An unexpected gust from the west almost knocks them off the road. This allows Joseph to turn his head to the right so he can look directly down the road with his left eye. There is no dust.

Joseph pulls back more of his protective cover, opens both eyes, and looks around. To his left (east) a boiling wall of dust rises from the ground through the bases of the clouds. The wall of dust is retreating to the east in the face of the west wind. The west wind is just as strong but it is blowing from the sea, not the desert.

Joseph pulls Mary up to his side and yells. "Open your eyes. We made it."

They pick up their stride and walk side by side, Joseph carrying his packs and Mary carrying Jesus.

CHAPTER 21

THE MISSION FAILS

G37 is walking beside the third spy in command of the ten soldiers of Herod's palace guard. He decided to join the party (although the spy doesn't know it) so he can witness the arrest of Joseph, Mary, and Jesus. It will be the culmination of his efforts to uncover the secret hiding place of the Prince.

The group marches into Bethlehem. The wind is still strong and gusts are blowing puffs of dust along the streets. No one is on the streets yet. The spy divides the palace guard into two groups of five. One group proceeds down the backstreet to the location of the agent behind Joseph's house. The other group follows him down the street to meet the second spy at the front of the house. That group takes G37 back to his old surveillance route.

The first group arrives at the location of the third spy. Having to face the wind all night has been brutal and the man is barely alive. Mud and dirt are caked around his eyes. At times he had to take shelter behind the wall but, when the wind shifted and drove the dust storm to the east, he was back at his post. The spy leads the guard through the gate into the backyard to position them to capture fleeing occupants.

Having the wind at his back, the second spy has fared better. The first spy, G37, and the five palace guards approach him. "Any activity?"

"None! Not at the house. Not on the street."

With a nod, the palace guard crosses the street. Bam! Bam! Bam! "Open this door!"

Again. Bam! Bam! Bam! "Open this door!"

Again. Bam! Bam! Bam! "By the authority of King Herod, open this door!"

Silence.

The leader turns to two larger men. "Break down this door!"

The two men push the door forcefully. The door gives slightly then stops. They slam against the door with full body weight. The door does not open. "Can't break it open. Must be barred from the inside."

The leader calls to the men standing in back. "Hey back there!"

"Yo!"

"The front door is barred. Break in the back."

After some "bams" and "thuds" a voice from the back calls out. "Can't get it open. Door is barred back here also. They must have barricaded themselves in."

The man in front shouts at the door; "By the authority of King Herod, I command you to open this door. We know you are inside. Now! Open this door!"

Silence.

People in the surrounding houses hear the commotion but are afraid to come outside. Some of the guards are cursing. "I guess we'll have to chop down the door;" grumbles one.

"Maybe not," replies the leader. "We can go through the window."

The window is too small for a grown man to crawl through. However, a child can do it. The leader orders his four men to search neighboring houses for a child of suitable size while he breaks open the window. Moments later the guards return with a screaming, crying child. The child is pushed through the window. Moments later there is a "thud."

The men push through the door with such force they knock the child backward and to the floor. They rush past the child into the second room and remove the bar from the door. The door swings open and there are six men inside and two outside both front and back.

"There's nobody here," calls one of the men.

Says another, "Doors were barred from the inside. It's like they vanished into thin air."

"If they aren't in the house then they must be hiding underneath it!" barks the leader. "Check for an underground passageway! You outside, check the roof."

The men pull out their swords and thrust them into the dirt floor. Where the dirt is hard-packed and can't be penetrated very far, the dirt has remained undisturbed for a long time. The guards are looking for soft dirt, broken dirt, which may overlie a hidden door in the floor.

Nobody here! Barred from the inside! Vanished into thin air! Lines appear in G37's brow. He must talk to somebody.

G37 departs in search of H99 and H307. There are drifts of dirt everywhere. He finds them not far away between the main road and the marketplace.

"Were you on duty last night?"

"As much as possible. The noise was more than our ears could bear so we retreated inside during the worst of it."

"That's not the issue," retorts G37. "Power shifts. The storm has no effect on power shifts. Were there any power shifts last night?"

"No! Nothing!"

G37 returns to Joseph's house, watches and listens as the guards work, then departs with haste. He has to get to the old warehouse in Jerusalem!

G37 stands before Z1. T18, T33, and S11 stand nearby.

"When the guards broke in, they found the house empty. That leads us to three possibilities. First the Father of the Prince sent angels and they vanished into thin air. Second Joseph and Mary hid with the Prince in a cave under the floor. Third, though it is difficult but can be done, Joseph rigged the bar to fall into place as they fled giving the impression that they did not intend to return."

"What is your conclusion?" demands Z1.

"I found H99 and H307. They witnessed no power shifts during the storm. That rules out the first possibility. The guards tested almost every inch of the floor inside the house in both rooms. There is no cave. That rules out the second possibility. That leaves the third possibility."

"If they intended to flee Bethlehem why do you think Joseph would have rigged the bar to give the impression that they did not intend to return?"

"An attempt to flee Bethlehem with a small child during that storm would have been suicide. I think Joseph wants us to think he fled so he barred the doors to give the impression he planned not to return. I think someone in Bethlehem is hiding them. After the guards leave, Joseph can reenter his house with the services of a small child just as the guards did."

Z1 turns away, facing the wall, with his hands on

his hips. G37 watches his hands slowly close, gripping and twisting the fabric of his garment. Z1 violently turns back around, his face red with rage. "Kill them!" he shrieks. "Kill them all!"

Not far away in another part of Jerusalem the spies and the guards stand before Herod. After hearing their accounts, he turns away toward the wall with his hands on his hips. His hands slowly close, gripping and twisting the fabric of his robe. Then Herod violently turns back around, his face red with rage. "Kill them!" he shrieks. "Kill them all!"

CHAPTER 22

FOUR PILGRIMS

Mary and Joseph have walked for two days. Joseph is not familiar with the area south of Bethlehem so he has no idea where the road goes except that it goes south. Also, he has no idea that the land here is sparsely populated and that is why he meets no other travelers on this road. One thing he does know from looking at local ecology is that the road descends in elevation. There are no longer any trees. There are shrubs but these have thinned out with time so that they are walking over rolling grasslands with shrubs mostly confined to dry basins. Finally, in the morning of the third day he meets a single traveler who tells him what he does not want to hear.

The road they are on does not go to Egypt. It continues south into the Negev. Once in the Negev, there is another road that goes to Egypt but that trip takes an additional seven days. At a brisk walk, it would take three days to get to the Negev road. That is a total of ten days to get to Egypt. Joseph does not have sufficient water or food to make a trip that long. Furthermore, there are few villages where he could purchase supplies.

The traveler does offer a hope, albeit a risky hope. In about a half-a-day walk there is a side road that cuts off and goes west to intersect with the highway to Egypt. That trip would take about two days. However, that road goes through rugged high country populated with robbers and highwaymen. Only the uninformed and the fools take that road.

After the traveler departs, Joseph and Mary discuss their options. The road they are on takes too long; the side road is too dangerous; or they can turn back. Mary insists that turning back to Bethlehem is not an option. "Besides," she smiles. "Maybe we belong on that dangerous side road. We are outlaws now."

Joseph is not humored. Besides, a while back, the road had topped a ridge, giving Joseph a wide view of the country. Looking back a long way up the road he had spotted four tiny dots. Herod would have soldiers out looking for them, and, if not, there were bounty hunters in his pay.

They crest another ridge, giving Joseph another opportunity to look back. The four travelers are much closer and Joseph can see their heads bobbing back and forth as they maintain a pace faster than Joseph and Mary can do, especially while carrying a two-year-old. Mary turns to Joseph. "We are being followed, aren't we?"

"Yes, four men are following us. But that doesn't mean they are hunting us."

It is now late in the afternoon. Joseph's and Mary's shadows are long across the road. They have not yet found the side road described by the lone traveler they had met earlier in the morning. Exhausted, they find a place of level ground cut back into the hillside about twenty feet or so and maybe forty feet wide. It is in the shape of a "U" with the opening facing the road. Scattered boulders make it a good place to sit or rest, but it offers little protection from the road.

"What are we to do about the men on the road?" asks Mary.

"Not much we can do. Let's just sit here and rest and not look up when they come by. Maybe they will ignore us and keep going."

Now they can hear a faint voice. Seems like it is a word being repeated over and over, like someone keeping time.

Hey…hey…hey…hey…hey…hey…hey. Joseph can clearly see the men. They carry loads on their backs. They are dressed alike in garments, maybe of burlap and of a tan color. Their heads are covered and they wear protective covering over their noses and mouths. Swords are at their sides. Hey…hey…hey… hey… hey…hey…hey. They walk in cadence in a line each about two steps behind the other. The first man is looking straight ahead and looks to pass by without notice. The second man is calling the cadence. Hey… hey…hey…hey…HO! The men stop directly in front of Joseph and Mary. The second man removes his protective clothing, revealing a handsome young man – dark hair, large brown eyes, a face chiseled like that of an athletic runner.

"You look famished!"

Joseph mumbles, "We are very tired."

"How is your water holding out?"

"We have some but not enough."

"Bathar. Do we have water to spare?"

"I believe we do."

The third man steps forward and removes his pack while Joseph hands up the partially-filled wineskin. The man lowers a spout and water pours into Joseph's wineskin filling it to the brim.

"Do you have any empty water skins?"

"Er, yes." Joseph quickly locates the empty wineskin and hands it up to the man. As the man fills it to the brim, Joseph looks at Mary and Mary looks at Joseph. Then Bathar closes his spout and stands back.

The leader turns to Joseph. "It is becoming dark. With your permission, we would like to camp here with you tonight. We can offer protection."

Before Joseph can reply, Mary says, "We would be delighted for you to stay."

The men lower their packs. "By the way, my name is Nathan. Bathar you already know."

Bathar bows slightly. Pointing to the fourth man; "this is Hildone." Hildone nods and gives a salute. Nathan points toward the first man, "and this is Feuryck, but we call him Fury for short." The first man gives a short bow.

Bathar and Hildone remove their head and face clothing revealing two handsome young men much like Nathan. Meanwhile Feuryck sits on a boulder closer to the road. The group unpacks. Finally Nathan turns to Feuryck. "Come on, Feuryck. Be sociable!"

Feuryck removes his head covering and unwraps his facial protection. He does not look like the others. His face is scarred and looks as if the muscles that form it have been cut loose and now hang down making his face round. His lips turn down at the corners leaving him with a permanent scowl. Instinctively Mary recoils and with her right arm draws Jesus closer to her.

Jesus laughs. Mary and Joseph freeze in fear. Then Nathan, Bathar, and Hildone start laughing. Finally the edges of Feuryck's lips begin to curl up. The smile slowly gets larger. Then an amazing thing happens. In a marvelous display of symmetry all the scars on his face line up to magnify his smile. Everyone laughs.

Now it is totally dark. Jesus is asleep. One of the men retrieves an oil lamp from his pack, removes the stopper, inserts a wick, and lights the lamp. It is a welcome source of light.

"How long have you been traveling?" asks Nathan.

"Three days now," replies Joseph.

"Where are you going?"

"Egypt. How about yourselves?"

"We are from north of Galilee. Every few years we take a pilgrimage to Egypt. Have some friends down in the Valley of the Kings."

"If you have traveled to Egypt before, why are you on this road?"

"Because Nathan had a bright idea," interrupts Bathar. "We got caught in a dust storm, so, rather than come into the high country where he thought the storm would be worse, Nathan suggested we take another road out of Jericho. That road took us down the Great Valley. When we figured out we were going the wrong way, Nathan found us a shortcut. The shortcut turned out to be a two-day hike on an animal trail – animals, by the way, that must thrive on steep terrain, and that brought us to this road."

"This road doesn't take us to Egypt," follows Joseph.

"Surely somewhere it connects with a road that does!" exclaims Nathan.

"True. But it is two days from here to that road, then seven days more to Egypt. At least that is what a traveler told us."

"Wow! That's a long way!"

"The traveler said there is a shortcut," interrupts Mary.

"Shortcuts! We are into shortcuts!" rumbles Feuryck's deep voice.

"But only fools go there," continues Mary. "The traveler told us the road goes through a place called 'Canyon of Robbers' and nobody gets through unseen, day or night."

"Sounds fun to me," rumbles Feuryck.

"I think we can take care of ourselves and you, if you choose to go with us," replies Nathan as he places his hand on the sword by his side. "Besides, Feuryck is a master swordsman."

Feuryck nods and smiles slightly.

"Perhaps it's time to get rest," offers Nathan. "Feuryck will take the night watch."

"Is Feuryck going to keep the watch for the whole night?" protests Mary.

"He will unless he doesn't want to. If he gets tired, he can come back and wake up one of us."

Feuryck rises, puts on his outer garment, picks up his sword and disappears.

Nathan puts out the light.

CHAPTER 23

HEY HEY HOREAY

When Joseph and Mary awake, it is already morning. Breakfast is prepared. The four men are repacking. Nathan approaches Joseph. "Feuryck scouted the road last night. The side road is only about thirty minutes away."

It takes longer than expected to get to the side road because of a fussy two-year-old who would rather walk than be carried. Finally, they stand at the entrance to the side road. Nathan comes close and looks down at Jesus. "Hey, Big Fellow. With your mother's permission, how would you like to ride on my shoulders for awhile?" A relieved Mary happily approves.

They walk as a mixed company. Feuryck is about two steps in the lead. Hildone is at the end. The road starts up what looks much like a flat plain centered over a dry creek bed. Low grassy slopes flank the plain on either side. As they walk, the grassy slopes seem to rise faster than they do. The slopes become higher, steeper, and closer in. Then rocky outcrops appear. As they round a curve, the slope on their side of the creek bed becomes a steep rocky wall. The opposite side is a confusion of rocky outcroppings mingled with large boulders. It is a perfect place to hide.

Feuryck raises his hand and the group halts. After some discussion Nathan turns to Joseph and Mary. "This is where Robbers' Canyon begins. Feuryck will go twenty paces ahead of us. Then I will follow. Jesus can ride on my shoulders but, if there is trouble, I will have to put him down. Joseph, you follow me to receive Jesus, if necessary. Then Mary will follow Joseph, and then Bathar will follow Mary. Hildone, you follow Bathar by about five paces." Each person finds his place and the walk up Robbers Canyon begins.

Joseph falls back far enough so he can see around Nathan ahead to Feuryck. After awhile Feuryck brandishes his sword and holds it in front of him. Then he holds the sword up waving it around. Nathan shows no alarm. As Feuryck waves his sword, sunlight glints off the blade in blinding flashes of light. Once, as Joseph looks on, the blade looks not at all like metal, but fire.

Feuryck disappears around a curve. As the rest of the party approaches the curve, out of the corner of his eye, Joseph thinks he sees movement on the other side – men, not hiding, nor attacking, but clambering over rocks and running away.

As the rest of the party rounds the curve, Feuryck is again in view, sword waving in the air. Now the sword is resting on his shoulder and Joseph hears his deep trumpet voice faintly. He appears to be chanting. Joseph doesn't understand the language. The chant goes something like "Hey, hey, horeay." Now the sword is waving in the air, the chant continues; "Hey, hey, horeay." Now his body is swaying; "Hey, hey, horeay." He just turned a complete circle! "Hey, hey, horeay." The man is dancing as he walks up the road! Any chance of getting through Robbers' Canyon unseen is lost!

Now others in the group are catching it. From behind, Joseph hears Bathar's voice; "Hey, hey, horeay." Nathan, with Jesus on his shoulder is swaying. These guys are chanting, singing, and dancing through the Canyon of the Robbers! Perhaps the place is not as dangerous as the traveler would have had him believe. They dance past what looks like an abandoned dwelling. However, Joseph cannot see the two men inside, bodies pinned against the inside wall staring at each other in terror.

Robbers Canyon is behind them. They crest the main ridge of the high country and are descending toward the plains that lead all the way to the Mediterranean Sea. Now late in the second day, with shadows lengthening rapidly, they round a curve and there, ahead about two miles, is the highway to Egypt.

The night's rest, refreshment, food, and drink behind them, the group is standing beside the Jerusalem-Egypt highway. Traffic is heavy. Many are on foot but there also are horses, camels, donkeys, and especially, long mule trains. Joseph and Mary are watching a merchant and his servant manage a train of ten mules on their way to Egypt. Nine of the mules are loaded with baggage, but the tenth mule carries nothing at all.

The mule train stops. Standing in the way are Nathan and Feuryck. Certain of a shakedown, the merchant is pleading to be spared. After Nathan quiets him, he speaks.

"Mister Merchant, we would like to offer you a proposition. We will give you protection. With us in charge, no one will steal your goods, attack your team, nor charge you for passage, all the way to Egypt. In return, we would like to seat this woman and her child on your unused mule. They have come a long way."

The merchant, transformed from losing everything to keeping everything, readily agrees. With a wave from Nathan, Joseph and Bathar help Mary and Jesus board the mule. Then Bathar waves back to Nathan. Nathan turns to the merchant while pointing to Feuryck. "Follow that man."

For about two hours their ride is uneventful. Then Feuryck's body begins to sway. "Hey, hey, horeay." He is dancing and turning in circles. Now it's beginning to catch on. "Hey, hey, horeay." Nathan, on the shoulder side of the road next to the animals and about a third of the way back from the front of the caravan, picks up the chant, his body swaying. Then Hildone, walking behind the caravan, dances and turns in circles. "Hey, hey, horeay." Joseph is pleased that Bathar, walking beside him omits the dancing part.

Fear rises in the merchant's heart. Just ahead of his caravan, nine or ten scruffy men stand at the edge of the road. "Hey, hey, horeay." Feuryck does not seem to notice as he is absorbed in his chanting and dancing. *Surely they will attack!* the thought rushes through the merchant's mind. "Hey, hey, horeay." Feuryck dances closer and the men take a step back from the road. "Hey, hey, horeay." The men step back again. Feuryck dances closer. The men step back further then leave the road entirely.

Wow! There must be something to this, thinks the merchant. "Hey, hey, horeay." He begins to chant and turns a full circle while dancing. "Hey, hey, horeay." To Joseph the sound seems to be coming from everywhere and from more than four men!

"Hey, hey, horeay."

A man on a passing camel turns toward Joseph: "Hey, hey, hooray."

Joseph is astonished. These four men, who have taken them under their wing, have succeeded in transforming the Jerusalem-Egyptian highway into one gigantic musical!

CHAPTER 24

BITTER MOURNING

They are in Egypt, a short distance inside the border. The merchant begs Nathan, Feuryck, Bathar, and Hildone to stay with him but they are continuing their pilgrimage to the Valley of the Kings by a different way. Joseph and Mary plan to stop in a burgeoning community of non-Egyptian nationals nearby. Mary hugs each of the men in a gesture of deep gratitude. Nathan hoists Jesus onto his shoulders and Feuryck frames a world-stopping smile, scars and all. Joseph thanks the four for supporting them during the journey, although it did take awhile to get used to the incessant singing, chanting, and dancing. With laughter at that, they part ways.

Joseph and Mary locate a vibrant community of Jewish people within the larger foreign community. They use proceeds from the sale of the Myrrh and spend some of the gold to secure housing. With aid from local leaders, Joseph finds plenty of work as a carpenter. Mary locates local markets and finds common ground with neighboring women facing the trials of raising toddlers.

Mary, with Jesus now three years old, is in the market place. She encounters a vendor selling small highly colored jars. "How much are these jars?" she inquires.

The vendor quotes a price. Mary looks over the jars counting thirty of them. "If I bought all thirty jars, would you give them to me at half price?"

The vendor agrees. Mary takes home thirty small perfume jars.

Now the container of frankincense is too large to be marketable except to the wealthy, who are few in number in their community. So, she transfers the resin into the thirty jars. A few days later, she and several of her friends return to the market place and set up business. By the end of the day all thirty of the jars are sold and Mary returns home with twice as much as she would have gained from selling the large jar of frankincense.

Joseph is prospering. His work schedule is similar to that in Bethlehem. He rises at dawn, has something to eat, and is on the road by sunrise. His new community is spread over the flat Red Sea/Nile River/Mediterranean Sea plain so it takes longer to walk to his work sites and it takes a lot more physical exertion to carry his tools and supplies. The physical effort is taking a toll on him and he hopes that soon he will be able to afford an animal.

One of the favorite pastimes in the community is hearing of stories from back in Israel. Most of the citizenry of Joseph's community consist of merchants and jobseekers along with their families. But those most interested in news are some wrong-doers running from arrest and political refugees who have fled to Egypt for some reason. One of the rumors of interest is that the high priest, Eleazer, has died.

Joseph has purchased an animal. He has prospered and is able to slack off a little bit with the donkey sharing his load. As is his daily routine when he arrives home from work, he ties his animal next to the back door. He releases his backpack with intent to carry the pack and tools inside and then return to unload the burden from the donkey. As he releases his pack, he hears the faint sound of a woman sobbing. Joseph rests his pack against the wall and goes inside.

Joseph finds Mary sitting by the table sobbing uncontrollably. Jesus stands quietly beside her with a hand on her lap. "Mary!" Mary looks up, her eyes bloodshot and her cheeks stained with tears. She resumes sobbing. "Mary, Mary, what has happened?"

Sob, "Rachel," sob, "Salome," sob, sob, "gone."

"Mary, tell me, what has happened?"

"Sob, sob, "Martha," sob, "Sarah," sob, sob, "Miriam," sob "all gone," sob, sob, "Bethlehem," sob, sob, "all gone."

It takes awhile for Joseph to piece together the events from the bits of information pried from Mary. One morning King Herod's army surrounded Bethlehem. The soldiers marched through the village routing out families from every house. Then they systematically butchered every male child younger than two years old. "When did this happen?" pried

Joseph, anger building inside.

Joseph sits down on a bench next to a wall, his jaw hanging down. The massacre happened two days after they fled Bethlehem in the dust storm. So that was why Joseph saw no soldiers all the way to Egypt. On the road out of Bethlehem he had feared the approach of the four men, Nathan and his friends, because he thought they might be under the pay of Herod. On the Jerusalem-Egypt highway he had feared that the incessantly loud behavior of Feuryck would draw too much attention their way. And when they approached the border with Egypt, he feared there would be guards. But there were none!

Joseph's anger gives way to a deep bitterness. *They were after Jesus! Herod's men slaughtered the male babies of Bethlehem thinking that, in doing so, they would certainly kill Jesus! If we hadn't fled, we would have been arrested and none of this would have happened. It is all our fault! No, wait, it isn't our fault. We are not criminals! We have done nothing wrong!*

Joseph looks over at Jesus. *This is an act of war! They are not at war with us. I am a nobody. Mary is a nobody. Jesus is a baby. No, wait! Jesus is the Son of God! This is an act of war against God!* The burden on Joseph's heart lightens as he remembers how precious is the cargo he has been given to carry. *A war against God! A war being fought on a dimension I don't understand!*

Joseph looks to Mary and his thoughts continue. *We are alone again. Mary is alone again. This is worse than Nazareth! No wonder she is mourning so bitterly. It would have been bad enough if one of her five friends had lost her son. All five lost their sons! But that is not all. Mary has lost her five friends! We cannot go back to Bethlehem! How can these five women who have lost their sons see Mary as a friend when, in their eyes, their sons are dead on account of Mary and her Son?*

CHAPTER 25

JOURNEY HOME

Mary opens a window. It seems the sun shines brighter and birds sing louder. People are calling to each other across the street. Good news! Some are cheering. King Herod is dead!

It is time to return to Judea. Joseph sells all but the essentials needed to make the trip. He picks some of his choice tools so he can make the transition into carpentry as quickly as possible once they arrive at their destination. The donkey is loaded with food, water, and other needed supplies. Joseph and Mary carry backpacks of bedding and other clothing. Jesus, now four going on five, gets to carry a backpack of some of

His clothes. They say goodbye to friends remaining in the community and, after several hours of walking, depart Egypt.

The road is crowded and, for three days, the trip is uneventful. Many travelers are returning home thanks to the timely departure of Herod. On the fourth day out, about mid-afternoon, they hear a deep trumpet voice coming up from behind. It is the voice of Feuryck. They stop for a joyful reunion.

The four men have completed their sojourn in the Valley of the Kings and are making their way back to their region north of Galilee. Would Joseph and Mary mind if the four pilgrims tagged along?

The men seem more deliberate or distracted or, in some way, troubled, as if things weigh heavily on their minds. There is no chanting, singing, or dancing on the highway as had happened on the trip to Egypt. Jesus gets to ride on Nathan's shoulders and Nathan makes a point of telling Him how much bigger and heavier He has become.

Jerusalem is in sight – a welcome sight. From there they turn onto the road to Jericho. There is a lot of traffic but not as heavy as on the road to Jerusalem.

After two hours they come to the junction with another road. Mary walks to the edge of the Jericho road and stands in the middle of the other road, facing Bethlehem. Nathan, Feuryck, Bathar, and Hildone form a box about an arm's length around her, protecting her from the oncoming traffic. Joseph and Jesus walk the donkey to the side of the road and look on. He notices Mary's shoulders heaving slightly, and then she seems quiet. After several minutes she turns toward Joseph, followed by the four men. "Let's go home."

The road to Nazareth splits off the main road at the base of a hill on which the city sits. It is another sad departure as the four men seem to be the only friends Joseph and Mary have. Sadly, Mary asks, "Do you think we will ever meet again?"

"I imagine we will," smiles Nathan. "I imagine we will."

With Mary holding Joseph's right hand, Jesus at her side and Joseph holding in his left hand the lead to the donkey, they walk slowly up the hill into Nazareth. Nearly five years ago, Joseph, holding Mary's hand in his right hand and holding the lead to a donkey with his left hand, walked slowly out of Nazareth. Five years ago, they left with all their possessions on the back of a donkey; today they return with all their possessions on the back of a donkey. Yesterday they left as outcasts; today they return as outcasts. Aside from Jesus at their side, five years seem to add up to almost nothing. It is as if a piece of paper upon which five years of history have been written has been folded back so that the two edges meet.

Joseph and Mary and Jesus make their way up the main road toward the market place. Unseen by them are H99 and H307 who are walking toward them. The two agents walk past without giving them a second look.

CHAPTER 26

RECONCILIATION

"Let's get something to eat," says Mary. Joseph ties the donkey to a nearby post and the three of them walk slowly into the market place. Mary secures some fruits and baked goods while Joseph makes payment. They carry their prizes to a bench at the edge of the market place. As they sit, eat, and relax, the fatigue of the long trip settles in on them.

"Mary?" comes a familiar voice from behind them.

Mary jumps up so fast, pastries go flying and an apple rolls about five feet from the bench.

"Mother!" squeals Mary. The two women wrap each other in an unending hug while squealing and sobbing - this time with tears of joy. Then Anne frees herself enough from Mary's grasp to pull Joseph into the hug. Joseph is elated to see a joyful wife but doesn't quite understand what all this celebration means. Jesus, with His mother and father wrapped in Anne's arms, draws closer.

Anne then pushes Mary and Joseph aside, squats down, and pulls Jesus into a hug, bending Him backward. "And this is…?"

"Jesus," finishes Mary.

"Jesus! What a wonderful name!"

Anne releases Jesus, rises, and faces Mary and Joseph. "Welcome! Welcome! Welcome! You must come home with me!"

"But what about Father?" questions Mary.

"Your father is a changed man. I'll tell you more as we walk. But first, let's get out of the market place."

"I have to get the donkey," protests Joseph.

"Oh, leave him there. He will be OK. If anything gets taken, Eli will make it up to you."

"What happened to Father?" asks Mary as they depart the market place.

"Of course we knew when you departed for

Bethlehem. When he heard what King Herod had done to the children there, Eli changed. He realized that what you tried to tell us about becoming pregnant was true. Else Herod would never have done what he did."

They turn up the street where Mary lived.

"Eli became hard to live with. He became alternately angry, contrite, or depressed. Finally, he took two of his workers as guards and the three of them went to Bethlehem searching for you. He returned relieved, I think, at not having found you. By the way, where were you?"

"We have just returned from Egypt," replies Joseph.

Later that afternoon, Eli arrives home. On sight of Mary, he rushes to her wailing and sobbing and pulls her into a never-ending hug. Joseph experiences a repeat of their first encounter with Anne. When Eli recovers, he holds Mary at arms length and looks her in the eye. "Forgive me! Forgive me! I was so wrong! I didn't believe you! You among all of us were always so close to the Most High!"

Eli and Joseph and Jesus are all too happy to devour the dinner prepared by Anne and Mary. As they sit at the table, having finished eating, and savoring their joyous reunion, the conversation returns to the new family relationships. Eli speaks, "Joseph, I will do what I can to repair the relationship between you and Jacob."

"Thank you. I appreciate that. However, I ask you not to tell him anything about Jesus – who Jesus is."

"Why not? I think your father would be delighted to hear who Jesus is, just as I am."

"I remember Bethlehem. I have two sisters who can't keep a secret."

"But Herod is dead!"

"Herod's rule was never threatened. Herod was an old man when he killed the children. He must have known beforehand that he would be long dead before an infant King of the Jews rose to power. No, I caught a glimpse of something driving Herod, something more powerful than Herod, something at war with the Most High.

We must fly under the radar! Who Jesus is must be kept a secret!"

The room falls silent. Then Mary speaks, "Father, when you went to Bethlehem, do you remember the names of any of the women you met there?"

Eli's eyes narrow as of one in deep thought. He begins slowly, "I have tried not to remember what I saw in Bethlehem. It was such a sad place. A tragic time! No, I don't remember any names. I only remember a woman telling me that her only comfort was in knowing that Herod failed to kill the 'God Child'." Mary smiles slightly and bows her head.

EPILOGUE

After Bethlehem, the critical mission of the Order was shut down and the participants returned to their former tasks. Nevertheless, Z1 was never one hundred percent certain that Herod's action in Bethlehem finished the Prince. Neither was G37 fully convinced, as Joseph and Mary, whom he could recognize, were never found. Yet some twenty-six years passed during which nothing happened. There was no evidence for the presence of the Prince.

Regarding John, old Elizabeth died when John was four years old. Zechariah passed away when John was fifteen. As the only son, all of the family inheritance was left to John. However, it seemed

John never recovered from the death of his father. He became more withdrawn and preferred to be left alone. He wandered in the woods, sometimes for days. He seldom if ever cut his hair. And he abandoned the attire of his father, the clothes of the Levite priesthood, and preferred a garment made of camel hair.

One day John left his home village never to return. He vanished into the wilderness of Judea. In some respects, he behaved like a wild man, wearing a garment of camel hair and surviving on a diet of locusts and wild honey. It seemed as though the plans of the Prince had failed.

However, John was not alone. Unnoticed by John, H227 became his constant companion. H227 had done some thinking. If John really was to be the forerunner of the Prince, then someday John would become the forerunner of the Prince if, indeed, the Prince was still alive. And that was something Z1 might like to know.

John and H227 wandered in the wilderness for several years. Then one day John changed. He became determined in his actions and set his course for where the wilderness meets the Jordan River. There he found some fishermen and proclaimed to them in a loud voice, "Repent, for the Kingdom of Heaven is at hand!"

The fishermen panicked and ran to a nearby village. Curious, the villagers went to the river and found John. But John was not a madman; he was a man with a message – a message of urgency that was prophetic and strangely convicting. "The axe is already laid at the root of the trees. Therefore, every tree that does not bear good fruit is cut down and thrown into the fire!"

John didn't judge his listeners; he baptized them for a sign of repentance. Those who heard him and were baptized departed, not feeling guilty, but relieved. Word about John spread widely and John spent whole days standing in the river, preaching his simple message, and baptizing people.

H227, convinced that John was not returning to the wilderness, turned up at an old abandoned warehouse in Jerusalem. He had an audience with Z1, T7, T33, and S11. Though Z1 knew of the Prince's plans to take on the form of a man, he did not know how the Prince planned to carry out His mission. H227 reported that John was like a magnet drawing people into repentance.

Maybe John was the Prince. Maybe the events at Nazareth and at Bethlehem were just diversions as T7 insisted. According to T7, the prophecy of John being a forerunner does not necessarily mean that John and the Prince are two different persons. It could mean that John (the forerunner) and John (the Prince) are two different manifestations within the same person.

Although he found T7's arguments compelling, Z1 was not convinced. "There is another way to find out who John is." Z1 turned to S11, who so successfully corrupted the mind of King Herod. Through demonization (pride, jealousy, greed, etc.), S11 corrupted the minds of the new high priest, Annas, and his son, Caiaphas. "Send some of the priesthood to John. Have them ask the question."

H227 was back on station by the Jordan River when he saw the Pharisees and Sadducees approaching. So did John; "You brood of vipers. Who warned you to flee from the wrath to come?"

"Never mind the water, John. We want to know. Are you the Messiah or should we look for another?"

"As for me, I baptize you with water for repentance, but He who is coming after me is mightier than I, and

I am not fit to remove His sandals. He will baptize you with the Holy Spirit and fire."

H227 is back in Jerusalem. The discussion centers on how to uncover the identity of the Prince. There is no need to restart the Mission. The purpose of the Mission was to defeat the Prince while He was a Child. That opportunity is long past. Z1 decides to bring in G37.

For G37, the trail to the Prince went cold after Bethlehem. In search for a place to start looking, he decides to visit H227. He finds H227 sitting on the bank of the Jordan River watching a long line of men lined up to receive baptism from John.

Some say it thundered. G37 sees a brilliant flash of light descend from heaven like a lightning bolt. He sees the light touch a man, having just been baptized, and sees the man glow, at first around His head and then over His body. H227 also witnesses the power shift. Both agents, eyes wide, jaws dropped, look at each other and exclaim; "The Prince!"

H227 and G37 are back in Jerusalem. The discussion centers on ways to overcome and eventually destroy the Prince. Finally, Z1 silences them.

“I will have to face Him myself. Perhaps He does not yet fully realize who He is.”

AGENTS ASSIGNED TO THE MISSION OF THE ORDER

Z1	The Supreme Commander, Satan
T7	Master, assigned to decode biblical prophecy
T18	Master, head of internal security
T24	Master, international communications
T33	Master, head of espionage
T49	Master, assigned to maintain files on Jewish people
S11	Assigned to corrupt King Herod
S52	Assigned to monitor angelic activity
R87	Thug
R91	Thug
M4	Sentry
M187	Sentry
J9	File keeper; aid to T49
H70	Spy, Bethlehem
H84	Spy, Bethlehem
H99	Spy, village of Nazareth
H227	Spy, village of Zechariah
H30	Spy, village of Nazareth
H346	Spy, assigned to the Temple
H524	Spy, assigned to the Temple

H624	Spy, village of Zechariah
G37	Information gatherer and synthesizer
G60	Information gatherer and synthesizer
G166	Messenger
E19	(Spirit of) Infirmity
D1	(Spirit of) Murder
C39	(Spirit of) Paranoia
C20	(Spirit of) Insecurity
B16	(Spirit of) Jealousy

SCRIPTURE REFERENCES

Below is a list of Biblical passages that are either referenced, quoted, or paraphrased.

Chapter 1
- Daniel 2:31-45
- Daniel 9:25
- Isaiah 9:6-7
- 2 Samuel 7:12-17

Chapter 2
- Luke 1:5-23

Chapter 3
- Luke 1:17
- Isaiah 40:3-5
- Luke 1:15

Chapter 4
- Luke 1:59-63
- Luke 1:67-70

Chapter 5
- Matthew 1:18-25

Chapter 6
- Matthew 1:18-25

Chapter 7
- Luke 1:17
- Isaiah 7:14
- Matthew 1:18-25

Chapter 8
- Luke 2:1-6

Chapter 9
- Luke 2: 7

Chapter 10
- Luke 2:8-20

Chapter 11
- Luke 2:13-14
- Luke 2:15-20
- Luke 2:21
- Luke 2:22-24
- Luke 2:25-35
- Luke 2:36-38

Chapter 12
- Numbers 24:17

Chapter 13
- Luke 2:8-20

Chapter 14

Chapter 15

Chapter 16
- Numbers 24:17
- Matthew 2:1-2

Chapter 17
- Micah 5:2
- Matthew 2:3-8

Chapter 18
- Matthew 2:9-10
- Matthew 2:11-12

Chapter 19
- Matthew 2:9-10

Chapter 20
- Matthcw 2:13-14

Chapter 21
- Matthew 2:13-14

Chapter 22
- Matthew 2:14

Chapter 23
- Matthew 2:14

Chapter 24
- Matthew 2:15
- Matthew 2:16-18

Chapter 25
- Matthew 2:19-23

Chapter 26

Epilogue
- Matthew 3:1-12
- Matthew 3:13-17
- Matthew 4:1-11

ACKNOWLEDGMENT

I am grateful to the following for their critical reviews of the manuscript: Earl L. Grinols (professor and author), Anne B. Grinols (professor and author), Cheryl A. Barkley (church elementary director), and Micah F.L. Barkley (author).

I am also indebted to Jack McNeil for rendering the manuscript into book format and designing the cover.

The book would likely not have been written had it not been for the encouragement and editorship of my wife, Sue.

Made in the USA
Monee, IL
18 November 2020

48123490R00111